'He's my chil

'No, he's not,' _____,
needing to sow doubt, to make him leave them
alone.

'I've seen a copy of his birth certificate.' Luc
started to argue. 'The date alone—'

'No father was named on it,' she whipped back.
'I wrote *unknown*. After all, I was a bed-
hopping slut, remember?'

He flinched at the hit. 'I was wrong about that.'

She raised a derisive eyebrow. 'A bit late to
revise your opinion, isn't it?'

'I'm sorry. I should have believed you, Skye. I
know that now.'

She wrenched her gaze away from the
glittering apology in his. It didn't change
anything. Nothing could change the deep, bitter
hurts of the past, the grief, the hardships, the
loss of all he'd taken from her on that one life-
shattering night. And she would not let him
soften her up with a facile apology.

Initially a French/English teacher, **Emma Darcy** changed careers to computer programming before the happy demands of marriage and motherhood. Very much a people person, and always interested in relationships, she finds the world of romance fiction a thrilling one and the challenge of creating her own cast of characters very addictive. Emma is the award-winning Australian author of almost 90 novels for Mills & Boon® Modern Romance®. Her intensely emotional stories have gripped readers around the globe. She's sold nearly 60 million books worldwide and won enthusiastic praise:

'Emma Darcy delivers a spicy love story...a fiery conflict and a hot sensuality.'
—Romantic Times

Recent titles by the same author:

HIS BOUGHT MISTRESS
THE OUTBACK BRIDAL RESCUE*
THE OUTBACK WEDDDING TAKEOVER*
THE OUTBACK MARRIAGE RANSOM*

Outback Knights trilogy

THE ITALIAN'S STOLEN BRIDE

BY
EMMA DARCY

MILLS & BOON®

First published in Great Britain 2005
Harlequin Mills & Boon Limited,
Eton House, 18-24 Paradise Road, Richmond, Surrey TW9 1SR

© Emma Darcy 2005

ISBN 0 263 84143 X

Set in Times Roman 10½ on 12¼ pt.
01-0505-44966

Printed and bound in Spain
by Litografía Rosés, S.A., Barcelona

CHAPTER ONE

'REMEMBER Skye… Skye Sumner…'

It was a shock to hear the name, falling from his brother's lips in a laboured whisper. Luciano Peretti frowned at the dark anguish in Roberto's eyes. Why speak of *her* now? Why waste any time at all on *her* when time was so precious?

In a few minutes Roberto would be wheeled out of this intensive care cubicle for the surgery that might or might not save his life. A fifty-fifty chance, the doctors had told the family. Their parents were out in the waiting room with the priest and Roberto's wife because of his brother's request to speak to him alone, and it seemed crazy to bring up Skye Sumner—an old wound between them that Luc had long since set aside for the sake of family harmony.

'Water under the bridge,' he muttered, wanting to dismiss whatever lingering guilt Roberto felt over the betrayal involved. 'Forgiven and forgotten,' he added for extra assurance.

'No, Luc.' It obviously pained him to speak but the determination to get out what he wanted to say demanded respect for the effort. 'I lied. It wasn't Skye…in the photos. She was never with me…like that. I set it up…to get her out of your life.'

Not Skye?

Luc's whole body clenched in denial. It couldn't be true. It was too…monstrous! Yet why would

5

Roberto make such a statement, a confession of such destructive deceit, unless he wanted—needed—to clear his conscience?

And if what he said was true... Horror swept through Luc's mind, unlocking a sealed compartment of memories, letting loose the ghosts of intense hurt and fury, images of the damning photos that had driven him to cut Skye Sumner out of his life. Roberto having sex with her, the raspberry birthmark on her thigh, the long blonde hair streaming across the pillow, the distinctive bracelet—three circles of white, rose and yellow-gold—around her wrist.

Her face—the incredibly appealing face with joy always sparkling in vivid blue eyes, the sexy full-lipped mouth that had so many different smiles, the fascinating dimples that came and went—had been hidden by Roberto's head, bent low as though he was whispering something in her ear, but Luc had not doubted it was Skye. The hair, the long lissome legs, the birthmark, the bracelet...

Apart from which, Roberto had backed up the evidence, admitting to a *playboy dalliance* with her, belligerently stating he'd seen Skye first, and why shouldn't he have her when she was willing?

Willing to laugh with Roberto, flirt with him... Luc had dismissed it as just light-hearted fun between them, glad that Skye had felt comfortable with at least one member of his family. He'd actually felt grateful to his brother...until the photos had blasted him into a different reality.

Blinded by the unbearable images, he'd seen no reason to suspect a set-up, no reason to accept Skye's wild denials, no reason to believe her explanation that she'd mislaid the bracelet, then miraculously found it, no reason to think anything but she was a two-timing slut who'd enjoyed having both brothers.

'Why?' The word croaked from his throat—a throat that had tightened from a wild melee of surging emotions. 'I *loved* her, Roberto.'

He rose to his feet, hands clenched, barely able to contain the violence erupting in him. If his brother wasn't half-dead already, lying in front of him as white as the sheet covering his broken body...

'Why?' he cried again, struggling to understand such—such malignance. From his own brother whom he'd trusted...trusted ahead of Skye...because he was family and family honour meant his word was his bond. 'What satisfaction could it have given you? Destroying my love for her...'

Stabbing me so deeply in the heart, I've never let any other woman into it.

'Dad wanted her out.'

A judgement Luc had flouted.

'Not suitable.'

A ruling made.

A sad irony glittered through the pain in Roberto's eyes as he struggled to spell out the rest. 'He had Gaia...picked out for you.'

Gaia Luzzani, who had never sparked one bit of sexual interest in Luc. Gaia, whom Roberto had married, earning their father's approval and placing himself to eventually take over the Luzzani multi-million dollar construction business—a business that complemented the Peretti property development company. The irony was that the grandchildren so eagerly anticipated by both Italian families had not been born.

Gaia had suffered two miscarriages so far, and if Roberto died…

'I was…jealous of you, Luc. The oldest son. The favoured son. I wanted Dad…to turn to me…have confidence in me…'

Luc shook his head, not knowing what to answer. His mind was spinning, trying to put the pieces together. 'Doesn't matter,' he growled, dropping back onto the chair under the weight of crushing despair.

Life had moved on. Six years had passed and there'd be no getting back with Skye. She wouldn't have a bar of him after the way he'd brutally dismissed everything she'd said, rejecting everything she was.

And facing him was his brother who might die in the next few hours. What good would it do to rail against him when his thinking had been dominated by their father…their conniving, determined to get his own way father!

Luc brought his own will to bear on what had to be done now—let his brother be at peace with himself before the operation. He took a deep breath and spoke soothing words. 'I'm sorry if I made life difficult for you, Roberto…being the first son.'

'Not your fault.'

The struggle for more breath was dreadful to watch. Smashed ribs, so much internal damage from the car accident…it was a wonder Roberto was still alive. And conscious.

'Got to tell you—'

'You've said enough,' Luc cut in tersely, wanting to block out thoughts of Skye and determined to save his brother any more extreme distress. 'It's okay. I'll deal with it.'

'Listen…' His eyes begged patience.

Luc waited, hating having to watch Roberto dragging up the effort to say more.

'Skye…was pregnant…'

'What?' Luc's mind reeled again. His memory of her denied any sign of pregnancy and she certainly hadn't told him there was any chance of one. She'd been on the pill. Yet the certainty in his brother's eyes made Luc question, 'How do you know?'

'Her stepfather came to Dad…with proof.'

'Why not to me?'

'He was…after money.'

'Did he get it?'

'Yes. I don't know if Skye…had the child…but you might have one…somewhere, Luc.' Tears filmed the pain and his eyelids closed over them as he heaved for more breath and choked out, 'I leave none.'

'Don't give up, Roberto!' Luc commanded. 'Don't you dare give up! You're my brother, dammit, and I don't care what you've done or not done!'

A faint smile tilted his mouth. 'I liked it…when we were kids…and you were the leader, Luc.'

'We had a lot of fun,' he gruffly agreed.

'Sorry…the fun…got lost.'

'We can have more together, Roberto,' Luc promised, fighting the finality he felt coming from his younger brother. He reached out and grasped his hand, willing his own strong life-force into the broken body on the bed. 'You'll make it through the operation. I won't let you die on me.'

The faint smile lingered.

The hospital orderlies came to take Roberto to the operating theatre. Luc had to let go, get out of the way. He found himself hopelessly tongue-tied, wanting to say more, yet floundering in the face of imminent separation…possibly final separation. It was Roberto who spoke the last words between them.

'Find…Skye.'

CHAPTER TWO

SKYE enjoyed walking her five-year-old son home from school. Matt was always bubbling over with news of what he'd done: the activities in the classroom, praise he'd received from the teacher, games he'd played with his new friends. Today he was bursting with pride at having shown off his reading skills, having been asked to read a story to the whole kindergarten class.

'What was the story about?' she inquired.

'A rabbit. His name was Jack and…'

Skye smiled as he recounted every detail of the story for her. Matt was so bright, so advanced for his age. She had worried about him fitting in with other five-year-olds who had yet to learn what he had somehow absorbed just through her reading bed-time stories to him every night. But he was still very much a little boy at heart and loved having play-mates.

It was now a month since he'd started school—no tears from him at having to leave his mother for most of the day. Excitement had sparkled from his lively blue eyes as he'd waved her goodbye, more than ready to charge straight into the new adventure of a bigger world for him. So far it was proving a very happy one.

Much to her relief.

It wasn't easy being a single mother with no-one

close to advise her or simply listen to her concerns. Matt seemed well adjusted to their situation. In fact, he'd coped extremely well with it, rarely pestering her when she was working with clients. Though now he was at school with children from normal families…what was she going to say when he asked about *his* father? As he inevitably would.

For so long there had just been the two of them. Matt didn't remember his grandmother, who'd died only eighteen months after he'd been born. And Skye herself had been the only child of an only child—no aunts or uncles or cousins. Her pregnancy, having the baby, caring for her mother through the bouts of chemotherapy that had proved useless in the end…the friendships she'd made at university had just dwindled away. Then setting up her massage business…no time for making social contacts.

If she'd gone out to work…but she hadn't wanted to leave Matt to a baby-sitter or put him in day-care. He was *her* child. Best to work at home, she'd thought. However, it had been a very closeted life these past few years. A lonely life.

Now that it was opening up for Matt, she should start re-thinking her own situation, look at other options for her future, maybe complete the physiotherapy course she'd had to drop, put herself in the way of meeting a possible husband, a father for Matt.

They turned the corner into the street where they lived and Matt instantly broke off his school chatter, pointing excitedly as he cried, 'Wow! Look at that red car, Mummy!'

Her gaze had already jerked to it. A red Ferrari—instantly recognisable to her, having been driven around in one by Luc Peretti. It was like a stab to her heart seeing it here, opening up painful memories, especially as she'd just been thinking about a father for Matt.

'Could we get a car like that?' he asked, clearly awe-struck by its brilliant colour and racy style, as she'd once been.

'We don't need a car, Matt.'

Nor could she afford one. Paying the rental on their small, two-bedroom cottage, plus living expenses, ate up most of her income. What she saved was emergency money. In fact, given that this neighbourhood was very modest real estate, and relatively cheap because of being under the flight-path to Mascot Airport, she wondered why such a classy and extravagant car was parked in their street.

'Other Mummies pick up their kids from school in cars,' Matt argued.

Skye grimaced at the all-too-true comment. The comparisons were starting. She tried emphasising the positive side of their own situation. 'I guess those kids don't live so close to school, Matt. We're lucky, being able to walk and enjoy the sunshine.'

'It's not so good when it rains,' he pointed out.

'I thought you liked wearing your yellow rain boots.'

'Yes, I do.'

She smiled at him. 'And splashing in puddles.'

'Mmm...' His gaze darted across the street to the red Ferrari. 'But I like that car, too.'

Skye rolled her eyes to the seductive object of little boys' dreams and shock ripped through her, thumping into her heart, halting her feet, making her stomach contract with tension. The driver's door was open and the man emerging from the car...it couldn't be, her mind reasoned frantically.

Then he turned his head, looking directly at her, and it was. It was Luc Peretti! No mistaking those distinctively carved features, the hard handsome maleness of that face, the riveting, heavily lashed, dark eyes, the thick black hair dipping with a wave at his right temple, just as Matt's did.

Matt!

A wave of panic churned through the shock. Had Luc somehow found out she'd kept her baby—the money given to her not used for an abortion? But why look for a child who—in Luc's mind, she thought savagely—might not even be his? Not Roberto's, either, given he believed she was a bed-hopping slut.

He half-turned to close and lock the car door. Maybe she was panicking for nothing. One look... She and Matt were the only people walking nearby. He could have been checking them out before leaving his high-class car—harmless people, just a young mother escorting her son home from school.

She didn't look eye-catching with all her hair drawn into a single plait down her back, no make-up apart from a touch of pink lipstick, unremarkable clothes—just white cotton slacks and T-shirt, which she wore to work in. He might not have recognised her at all, might have parked in this street for some other reason entirely, not because *she* lived here.

'Mummy?'

She tore her gaze from Luc Peretti to look down at her son. 'Yes?'

'Why are we stopped?'

Because I'm frozen with fright.

Skye quickly drew in a quick breath and came up with, 'I've just remembered I've forgotten something.'

'What?'

'Something… I meant to do for a client. I'll do it tomorrow,' she said, desperately temporising as she frantically willed Luc Peretti to be walking away from them, setting her free from this dreadful inner angst.

'Better put it on your list,' Matt advised, grinning at her habit of making careful lists for everything. 'Then you won't forget.'

'I'll do that as soon as we get home.'

'Well, come on.' He grabbed her hand to urge her forward again.

Skye forced her feet to move. She had to look, to see where Luc Peretti was now. The jolt to her heart was worse this time. He was crossing the road to *their* sidewalk, watching them, his face set in grimly determined purpose. If Matt hadn't been tugging on her hand, Skye might have stopped dead again. As it was, she felt weirdly disembodied from her legs which kept pumping forward, matching her son's steps.

There was no avoiding a confrontation now, she told herself. Luc Peretti was clearly intent on one. Having reached the sidewalk, he moved straight to the front gate of their house and stood there waiting for them, his gaze trained on Matt as they walked towards them.

Looking for some likeness to himself, Skye thought, the panic rising again, making her dizzy with turbulent fears. The Peretti family was so wealthy. If Luc decided to make a claim on Matt…and God knew she'd had experience of them playing dirty, getting some woman to look like her in the photos, stealing her bracelet and returning it so she'd be wearing it when Luc came to accuse her…accuse her and dump her for an infidelity she'd never committed.

Ruthless people.

Cruel people.

Callous people, uncaring of the lives of others.

She fiercely told herself Luc couldn't be sure Matt was his child. Yes, he had olive skin, very dark hair and long thick eyelashes, but he also had her blue eyes, her mouth, and certainly her more sunny personality. Luc would have to get a DNA test to be sure. Could she refuse it, fight it?

'Do you know that man at our gate, Mummy?'

No point in denying it. Luc was bound to address her by name. 'Yes. Yes, I do, Matt.'

'Can I ask him for a ride in his red car?'

'No!' The word exploded from the volcano of fear inside her. She instantly halted and dropped into a crouch, turning Matt for an urgent face-to-face talk. 'You must never get in his car. Never go with him anywhere. Do you hear me, Matt?'

Her vehemence frightened him. She could see him trying to understand and her heart ached for the simplicity of their life which was being so terribly threatened.

'Is he a bad man?' His voice quavered, reflecting her alarm.

Was Luc bad? She had loved him once, loved him with an all-consuming intensity that had made his disbelief in her integrity totally devastating. Even now she couldn't bring herself to say he was bad, though he'd let himself be deceived by his family, making himself one of them, against her.

'You just mustn't go with anyone unless I say it's all right. No matter how much you want to, Matt.' Her hands squeezed his anxiously. 'Promise me?'

'Promise,' he repeated, troubled by her intensity.

'I'm going to give you the door-key now. When we get to the front gate, you go straight inside and wait for me. Have your milk and cookies. Okay?'

'Are you going to talk to the man?'

'Yes. I'll have to. He won't go away until I do.'

Matt shot a frowning look at Luc. 'He's big. I can call the 'mergency number for help, Mummy.'

She'd taught him that—a necessary precaution since she was the only adult in the house and if something happened to her… Skye tried to calm herself, realising Matt was picking up on her fear, wanting to fix what he sensed was a bad situation.

'No, there's no need for that,' she assured him. 'I'll only be a few minutes.' She took the door-keys out of her pants pocket and pressed them into his hand. 'Just do as I say, Matt. Okay?'

He nodded gravely.

She straightened up and they resumed their walk, hands tightly linked, mother and son solidly together. And let no one try to separate them, Skye thought on a savage wave of determination.

Luc had shifted his gaze to her, a dark burning gaze that made her pulse race and her inner muscles quiver. She lifted her chin high in a proud defiance of his power to affect her in any way whatsoever. The time had long gone when she had giddily welcomed him into her life, when she had so completely succumbed to his many seductive attractions.

He was big in Matt's eyes but in Skye's, that translated to powerful...tall, broad-shouldered, slim-hipped, a strong muscular physique with not an ounce of flab anywhere. He had the kind of perfect masculinity that automatically drew a woman's attention, looking strikingly sexy in any clothes, especially none at all.

He was wearing black jeans, no doubt with a designer label. A black sports shirt showed off the impressive width of his chest and the bared strength of his forearms. One hand was gripping the top of her gate, as though ready to block any escape from him.

He had no right to. No rights at all where she was concerned. And he still had to prove he had any paternal right to Matt. She glared furious independence at him, shifted her gaze pointedly to the trespassing hand, then back to him with a belligerent challenge. He dropped his hold on her property, moving the offending hand into a gesture of appeal.

'Could I have a word with you, Skye?'

The deep timbre of his voice struck more painful memories, how he'd used it to make her believe he loved her, intimate murmurs in bed, reinforced by how he'd touched her, kissed her. A flood of heat raced up her neck and scorched her cheeks—shame at having let him remind her of how it had once been between them.

She kept a safe distance, halting a metre away from him, a blazing demand in her eyes. 'Please move aside from the gate. I'll stay and have a word with you but my son needs to go inside.'

He opened it before stepping back, giving Matt free passage. 'I'd like you to introduce us,' he said, smiling down at the boy that might be his, pouring out all his Italian charm in case it was.

Steel shot up Skye's backbone. 'He's *my* child. That's all you need to know.' She released Matt's hand and nudged his shoulder forward. 'Go on now. Do as I told you.'

He obeyed, at least to moving past the opened gate. Then he stopped and turned, delivering his own childish challenge to Luc Peretti. 'Don't you hurt my Mummy!'

Luc shook his head, a surprisingly pained look on his face. 'I didn't come to hurt her. Just to talk,' he answered gently.

Matt glared at him a moment longer, then glanced uncertainly at Skye who gestured for him to leave them. Much to her relief, he did, running up the front path to the door. She watched him unlock it and close it behind him before she looked back at the man who had no right to be here. No moral right. And he had to know it!

'What do you want to say?' she clipped out, hating him for what he'd put her through, was putting her through now with this intrusion on their lives.

'He's my child, too, Skye,' he stated with not the slightest flicker of uncertainty in the darkly burning eyes.

'No, he's not,' she retorted vehemently, needing to sow doubt, to make him leave them alone.

'I've seen a copy of his birth certificate,' he started to argue. 'The date alone…'

'No father was named on it,' she whipped back. 'I

wrote *unknown*. After all, I was a bed-hopping slut, remember?'

He flinched at the hit. 'I was wrong about that.'

She raised a derisive eyebrow. 'A bit late to revise your opinion, isn't it?'

'I'm sorry. I should have believed you, Skye. You weren't the woman in the photos. I know that now.'

She wrenched her gaze away from the glittering apology in his. It didn't change anything. Nothing could change the deep, bitter hurts of the past, the grief, the hardships, the loss of all he'd taken from her on that one life-shattering night. And she would not let him soften her up with a facile apology.

Regathering her defences against the insidious attraction that could still tug at her, Skye swung her gaze back, hard and straight. 'How do you know it?' she mocked. 'Your brother was a starring player in those photos. Who better to believe?'

His jaw tightened. The expression in his eyes clouded, taking on a bleak distance. 'My brother… died…a month ago.'

Roberto dead?

So young?

The shock of Luc's flat statement completely smashed Skye's concentration on rejecting him as fast and as effectively as she could. An image of Roberto Peretti flew into her mind—a head of riotous black curls, wickedly flirtatious eyes, teasing smiles backing up his playboy charm, not as tall nor as solidly built as Luc, not as strikingly dynamic, but with a quick-silver energy that had instant appeal. She had liked him, laughed with him, but as far as serious attraction went, he'd always faded into insignificance beside Luc.

Roberto had been fun.

Until she'd seen him in the damning photos.

That reminder swiftly brought Skye back to her current crisis. 'I'm sorry for your loss, Luc,' she said stiffly. 'But it has nothing to do with me.'

'You were on his conscience just before he died. His last words were about you, Skye,' he said quietly.

So Roberto had confessed the truth, removing the totally undeserved stain on her character. And, of course, Luc would believe his brother's deathbed confession. 'It makes no difference,' she muttered.

'It does to me,' he shot at her.

'You don't count,' she flung back. 'You ceased to count for anything in my life a long time ago.'

He grimaced, sucked in a deep breath, then slowly nodded. 'Fair enough.' The concession was swiftly followed by more resolute purpose. 'But the fact of your pregnancy was kept from me until Roberto revealed it. And I now know there is a child to consider. *Our* child, Skye.'

'No. Mine!'

Everything within her revolted at any claim of possession from him. His ignorance of her pregnancy had no bearing on Matt's life—the life *she* had given Matt—the life the Peretti family had wanted to snuff out, along with all involvement with her.

Luc gestured an appeal for reason. 'DNA tests can prove—'

'Have you spoken to your father about this?' she cut in, needing to know if Luc was acting alone, without the backing of the very powerful and wealthy

Maurizio Peretti. The threat he embodied was bad enough, but if he had his father's approval to make this approach...

'It's none of his business,' came the terse reply.

'He made it his business,' Skye corrected him, relieved to be able to use her last piece of ammunition against any claim on Matt. 'Your father paid out a thousand dollars for an abortion. He killed *your* child, Luc.'

'No!' He shook his head, appalled at the accusation. 'He wouldn't do that. He'd *never* do that.'

'He did. So don't think you can resurrect a paternity issue six years down the track. My son is *my* son. I chose to have him.'

'Skye—' an anguished appeal in his eyes '—I had nothing to do with any of this.'

She hardened her heart against him. 'Yes, you did, Luc. You didn't believe me. You accepted what your family told you. Go back to them and the life they planned for you. You're not wanted here.'

The gate was still open.

He was clearly in shock over what she had revealed.

Skye took the chance he wouldn't try to stop her. With bristling dignity she stepped past him, closed the gate behind her without so much as a glance at him and proceeded up the path to the front door, her ears alert to any sound that might indicate pursuit, her heart pounding hard with the fear of not making good her escape.

Matt had left the key in the door for her.

Good boy! she thought in fierce relief.

Her whole body was tense, expecting a call or some

preventative action from Luc, but it didn't come. She unlocked the door, moved into the protective shelter of the house and closed out the man who should never have re-entered her life.

It wasn't fair.

It wasn't right.

Luc Peretti could only bring her more grief.

CHAPTER THREE

Luc barely controlled a burning rage as he drove up the grand carriage loop to the neo-Gothic mansion his father had bought at Bellevue Hill. Twenty million dollars he'd paid for it five years ago, and he could probably sell it for thirty now, given its heritage listing and commanding views of the Sydney Opera House and Harbour Bridge.

Twenty million for a piece of personal property.

Next to nothing for a grandson!

Paid off, Roberto had said. That hadn't added up to Luc when the private investigator had found Skye and her son living in a cheap rental at Brighton-Le-Sands. She hadn't even completed her physiotherapy course, working as a masseur to make ends meet. No car. No credit rating. No evidence of a nest-egg account anywhere.

He'd wondered if she'd torn up his father's cheque, scorning to take anything from a family who'd made her out to be little better than a whore. Her whole demeanour this afternoon had been stamped with steely pride, determined on rejecting anything he offered. Their child was *her* son. Hers alone. Sold to her for a thousand dollars—a measly thousand dollars!

Luc still could not bring himself to believe his father had paid her that sum for an abortion. Such an act was totally against Italian culture and Maurizio

Peretti was nothing if not traditionally Italian. He might want an unwanted bastard child to disappear, especially if it could become a glitch in the Peretti-Luzzani master plan, but demanding its life be ended?

No.

Nevertheless, Luc was determined on confronting his father with the accusation, given Skye's belief in it.

He'd lost her—lost five years of his son's life—because he hadn't believed her. He was not about to repeat that mistake. Let his father answer for what had been done. And not done. Maybe then the truth could be pieced together.

He brought the Ferrari to a crunching halt at the front entrance to the huge sandstone home. Forty-five rooms, he thought derisively, more than enough to house a large extended family in the grandeur his father's ambition demanded. Roberto would have obliged with the desired grandchildren, but Roberto was dead and his childless widow had returned to the bosom of the Luzzani family for comfort. The nursery rooms were empty. So many rooms empty.

Luc felt the emptiness echoing all around him as he walked down the great hall to the sitting room his mother favoured. She was occupying her usual armchair, dressed in mourning black, drowning her sorrows with Bristol Cream Sherry as she watched the early evening news on television.

'Where's Dad, Mamma?' he asked from the doorway.

She didn't turn her head. In the dull flat tone that characterised her every utterance since Roberto's death, she answered, 'In the library.'

No interest in him. No interest in anything. Luc doubted she even heard or saw the news being reported. None of it impinged on her very protected life. But great wealth could not protect against miscarriages nor accidental death. Nor could it provide solace for the loss of her beloved younger son and all his life had promised.

He left her and moved on, bent on pursuing his own needs which were far more imperative right now. Besides, he remembered only too well his mother had not approved of Skye. If she had been in on the conspiracy, too... Luc gritted his teeth against the wave of violence that churned through him.

The machinations that had taken place behind his back were a dark ferment in his mind—a ferment he had to contain while he listened and observed, weighing whether he could even keep on being involved with his parents. Certainly, in Skye's mind, his family was *the enemy* to any future he might forge with his son. And she had no reason to think otherwise.

He entered the library without giving a courtesy knock on the door. His father sat at a magnificent mahogany antique desk, tapping at a pocketbook computer he carried with him everywhere, probably checking up on any movement in his investments. His agile brain kept track of an incredible array of figures which he could rattle out at any pertinent moment.

Luc had always admired his father—a formidable go-getter who knew what he wanted and went after it, using every resource he could pull into play. Maurizio Peretti had friends in politics, friends in the church, friends in many high places, all of them impressed by what he could do for them, and, of course, the occasional favour was asked and given in return.

But it wasn't just his accumulated wealth that impressed them. It was his business acumen and a charismatic presence that shouted leadership quality; the tall, powerful physique, the almost mesmerising intelligence in the commanding dark eyes, the thick thatch of wavy iron-grey hair, the hawkish nose, and the mouth that never spoke rubbish.

He looked up from his notebook, surprise and pleasure instantly lightening the air of deeply focused concentration. 'Luciano! Glad you came by! Have you spoken to your mother?'

Family first… Luc's mouth curled in black irony. He'd give his father *family!* He crossed the room in a few quick strides and tossed the large envelope he carried onto the desk. 'Something requiring your immediate attention, Dad,' he drawled.

His father frowned at the disrespect implicit in Luc's manner. 'What is this?' he demanded curtly.

'Photos. Remember the photos you presented to me six years ago?'

The frown deepened. 'Why would you keep them?'

'I didn't. These are new photos, Dad.'

'I don't understand.'

'You will. Since you seem reluctant to look at them, let me help.' Luc snatched back the envelope, ripped it open, removed its contents and slapped the photos one by one, face up, across his father's desk. 'Skye Sumner with my son,' he declared in bitter fury. 'My son who is now a schoolboy. My son whose first five years of life I have missed because I did not know of his existence. Look at him, Dad!'

The passionate outburst drew no more than a shuttered glance at the photos and a stoney-faced defence. 'How do you know it is your son?'

Luc's arm flew out in a fiercely dismissive gesture. 'Don't come at me with that.' He drew himself up in towering contempt. 'Roberto confessed to your indecent conspiracy against Skye on his deathbed. He told me about the pregnancy, told me you'd paid her off. Don't even start denying it!'

His father's mouth compressed into a thin line of distaste. He sat back in his antique studded leather chair and viewed Luc through narrowed eyes, eyes that were weighing options for dealing with this crisis. 'Surely, in hindsight, you realise she was an unsuitable wife for you,' he stated unequivocally.

'Don't go there, Dad,' Luc warned, hard ruthless steel in his own eyes. 'You've lost one son. You're very close to losing another.'

'I did what I thought was best for you, Luciano,' he said, attempting a tone of appeasement. 'You were blindly infatuated—'

'I'm here to give you one chance—' Luc held up his index finger for pointed emphasis '—one chance to answer Skye's accusation that you paid her off with a thousand dollars to have an abortion.'

'That's a lie!' He exploded up from his chair, hurling his hands out in furious counter-challenge. 'You see what a scheming little bitch she is, trying to turn you against me? I paid out one hundred thousand dollars, with more to come when it was needed!'

'Then why doesn't she have any money?' Luc bored in. 'Why is she living in borderline poverty?'

'She must be hiding it.'

'No, she's not. Trust me on this. A thorough investigation has been done. There is…*no money!* In fact, she has no support whatsoever. Her stepfather did a flit while she was still pregnant. Her mother died of cancer when the baby was only eighteen months old. She was left with nothing but old furniture and she has survived—*with my son*—by building up a modest massage business.'

'Massage,' his father jeered, his eyes flashing a filthy interpretation of that profession.

Luc's hands clenched. He barely held back the urge to smash his father's face in. 'Remedial massage,' he bit out. 'A natural offshoot from the physiotherapy course she was doing at university when I knew her—a course she didn't—couldn't—complete with neither the money nor support needed to go the distance. So the evidence—*the evidence, Dad!*—is all against your having paid her off with anything more than the thousand dollars Skye claims.'

His father bristled with offended dignity. 'You doubt my word?'

'I have every reason to doubt your word where Skye Sumner is concerned,' Luc fired at him point-blank, not giving a millimetre.

His father's chin lifted aggressively. 'I can prove the money was given. And more to come.'

'Then start proving it!'

'The papers are at my solicitor's office.'

'Call your solicitor. Get him to bring the papers here. Show them to me…before you have the chance to cook up more lies behind my back.'

For several tense moments the air between them was charged with Maurizio Peretti's fierce pride and

Luc's explosive mistrust—a mistrust that Maurizio finally realised could destroy everything between them. He reached for the telephone and began dialling.

Needing to put a cooling distance between himself and his father, Luc moved over to one of the tall, narrow, lancet windows which gave a limited view of the east garden. Limited views was not only a problem with the old-fashioned architecture of this house. The limited view his father had of Skye Sumner was deeply offensive to him, especially since she'd been innocent of the damning sins manufactured against her. He wasn't sure he could ever forgive his father for that. If the solicitor couldn't bring proof of some caring…

'John, I'm sorry to break in on your evening but this is an emergency. I need the Skye Sumner file and I need it now.'

Silence while the other man spoke.

'Yes,' his father replied tersely. 'I'm at home. Bring it here as soon as you can.'

End of conversation.

Luc didn't turn around. He had nothing more to say to his father at this point and the tension inside him needed some calming. Seeing Skye in the flesh today, being in touchable distance of her…it wasn't only his son he wanted. Had he ever stopped wanting her?

It had driven him mad, seeing her with Roberto in the photos, thinking of her giving his brother what he'd believed was all his, only his, the gift of herself in loving abandonment. Somehow he had to persuade her she could trust him with that gift again. Somehow…

'A trust fund was set up for the child's support and education,' his father stated, the leather of his chair creaking as he resumed his seat behind the desk to wait for the solicitor's arrival.

If that was true, there could not have been an instruction to abort the child. Not from his father. Yet Luc would not disbelieve Skye. So where had the instruction come from? Had one of his father's underlings decided that cutting corners would be the best result for his boss?

'All she had to do was apply in writing for funds to become available,' his father went on tersely, hating being in a defensive position.

'Then why didn't she?' Luc challenged, not bothering to even glance over his shoulder.

No answer to that.

Luc deduced the solicitor had told his father the file had not been re-opened since it had first been set up. It was the only answer that made sense of what he knew about Skye's life. Certainly *she* was not aware of any trust fund.

There was a drumming of fingertips on the highly polished desk. Then came the first line of counter-attack to the accusation of irredeemable guilt where caring for a grandchild was concerned.

'I dealt with the stepfather. Everything was worked through him. You said he did a flit before she had the child. If what you say about her circumstances is true, he must have scammed the money and never told her about the trust fund.'

The stepfather…neatly removing all responsibility from himself. But not blame, Luc thought viciously.

None of this would have happened without his father's controlling hand behind it.

'Then you made a huge mistake of judgement in trusting him, didn't you?' he mocked. 'As well as not caring enough to check up on what was happening to *my child*.'

'Luc…' It was a brusque appeal, looking for some foothold on a meeting ground where he could twist around to regain some credibility.

'Let's wait for the file to arrive. That might…' He half-turned to stare long and hard at the man who had interfered so intolerably with what should have been. '…*might*…' he bit out warningly, '…go some little way to restoring a viable relationship between us.'

'You're my son. What was done was done for—'

'Don't say *for me*. You weren't thinking of me. Nor Skye. Nor our child. You were thinking of what *you* wanted. When you stop thinking of what *you* want and start respecting what I want, perhaps we'll have something to talk about.'

'I'm giving you what you want. I called John to bring you the proof…'

'Step One.'

His chin came up aggressively. 'What is Step Two?'

'You will immediately start revising your attitude towards Skye Sumner. If you speak once more of her in any kind of deprecatory manner, I will walk out and I won't come back.'

He grimaced but didn't argue. 'Is there a Step Three?'

'Step Three is full acceptance of her and our son in my life. That means no undermining act behind my back. And believe me, I'll know about it if you so much as raise a finger to interfere between us again.'

A giving gesture was waved. 'If you want to take an interest in the boy…'

'Not just the boy. I intend to do everything within my power to persuade Skye Sumner to marry me.'

Shock cracked the facade of appeasement. 'Surely there's no need for that.' The words whipped out of him. 'I can understand about the boy…'

The violence Luc had held in check erupted, his body jerking into action, his legs closing the distance between them so fast, everything was a blur except the need to punch home his point. His fist crashed down on the desk, making his father flinch back in his chair.

'Understand *me!*' His eyes blazed unshakeable resolution as he reinforced it with all the turbulent passion stirred by the situation. 'Skye Sumner should have been my wife. I want her as my wife. And I will have her as my wife.'

CHAPTER FOUR

NOTHING felt safe anymore.

Skye told herself that was another reason why she had to meet Luc Peretti this morning. Ever since the solicitor had come, showing her all the legal documents and the private investigator's report on her stepfather, she had been feeling the power of the Peretti family closing around her, squeezing for a claim on Matt. She had to find out what their aim was—the end goal.

Right from her first encounter with Luc two weeks ago, she'd been afraid he wouldn't just walk away. Now she knew he'd confronted his father and moved relentlessly to demonstrate how terribly deceived she'd been by her stepfather. But that didn't make the Peretti family right in what they'd done, she argued to herself.

Her pulse kicked in shock as she glanced at the clock and saw it was already nine-thirty.

She had to get moving.

A last check in the door mirror of her bedroom showed she had eaten off some of her lipstick, probably from nervously chewing at her lips. Her hand was shaking as she quickly replenished it. Stupid to worry about her appearance, she thought. It didn't make any difference to what would happen.

Luc's mother would probably sniff her disapproval of the cheap cotton sundress she wore, but she wasn't meeting Luc's mother and never would again. It had been the hottest summer on record in Australia and even though it was now mid-March, the weather still hadn't cooled. She had a half-hour walk ahead of her and the sundress should keep her from feeling overheated and sticky at the meeting with Luc.

She'd pulled her long hair into a clip at the back of her neck and she quickly jammed the wide-brimmed straw hat on her head, slid her feet into comfortable sandals, grabbed her sunglasses and handbag, and left the house, her heart fluttering uncontrollably over having to deal with the man who knew he was Matt's father.

At least, he hadn't asked for Matt to accompany her. In fact, there had been no threatening pressure attached to his request for a meeting, as relayed by the solicitor. The choice of time and place had been hers and it was to be just the two of them.

The request had seemed reasonable, the meeting necessary, given the dreadful fraud her stepfather had perpetrated, including forging her signature on some papers, using her pregnancy to extort the awesome sum of money from the Peretti family.

One hundred thousand dollars!

Her mind still boggled over it.

And the cheque Luc had written to cover the loss of it was burning a hole in her handbag. It had been attached to all the other papers the solicitor had left with her, but she couldn't keep it. Firstly, the money had been stolen by her stepfather, not by Luc. Just because it was irrecoverable didn't make it right for her to accept full replacement of it.

Besides, if she was to stick to her independent

stance, she had to return the cheque, and meeting Luc was the most direct, most telling way to accomplish it. She had to make it clear to him that *she* hadn't asked for money and didn't want it now. None of it. No way could she use the trust fund. It would tie Matt to the Peretti family, and she didn't believe that was a good connection for him at all.

Tainted money.

Better not to owe the Peretti family anything.

She could manage to bring up Matt by herself.

Skye bolstered this determination with every step she took towards the meeting place—the waterfront park, directly across from the Brighton-Le-Sands Novotel Hotel, a public area which she could check out before showing up. It was just on ten o'clock— her stipulated time—when she reached the hotel and hurried up to the first floor to take the overhead walkway spanning the busy coast road to the park. From there the whole area could be scanned.

She spotted Luc instantly, seated on a park bench under the shade of one of the Norfolk pines that skirted the shoreline. His head was turned towards the long runway at Mascot Airport where big jets were constantly landing or taking off. One arm was casually hooked over the back rest of the bench, making him look relaxed.

Skye certainly wasn't. The tension gripping her nerves was so bad, she paused to take several deep breaths, trying to calm herself. It was important to appear cool and confident, not get rattled. It was totally irrelevant that he was still the most attractive man she'd ever met, still able to tug at her physically. Luc Peretti and everything related to him had to be ejected from her life. With this resolution firmly fixed in her mind, she forced herself to walk on.

His gaze swung to her as she descended the steps on the park side of the walkway. Although her thighs started quivering, her legs kept carrying her down, driven by sheer willpower. He stood up, waiting by the park bench, watching her approach, his dark brilliant eyes keenly observing everything about her.

She was glad she'd armoured herself with sunglasses. Not only did they hide her thoughts and feelings, but they allowed her to return his scrutiny without being obvious about it. Again he was wearing casual clothes; beige cotton slacks, a loose cotton knit top in white and beige, V-necked, short sleeves—very smart, undoubtedly expensive, but not intimidating.

Skye surmised he hadn't come to throw his weight around. Or were the clothes another deception, meant to put her off-guard while he set up the big guns to attack her position?

His mouth twitched into a sensual little smile, making her acutely conscious that her sundress left a lot of flesh bare.

Was it possible he still found her desirable?

Her stomach curled at the thought.

Worse—her pulse-rate zoomed into overdrive as his smile widened and his eyes warmed with pleasure.

'Good to see you again, Skye,' he said with what seemed genuine sincerity.

Her mind jammed for a moment, then spun with wild speculation. Was this manner aimed at winning her compliance with whatever he wanted? Did he think she could forget how he'd spurned her? Casting her out of his life on the very night she'd meant to tell him she was pregnant with his child!

A surge of anger spilled into a bitter outpouring. 'I can't say it's good to see you, Luc. I only came to return your cheque. To place it in your hands personally so it *can't* get mislaid or misappropriated or mis...anything else.'

She started fumbling with her handbag, desperately eager to get the zippered compartment open, extract the cheque, get rid of the burden of Peretti money.

'Skye, you're owed child support for the past five years,' he argued in a gentle, soothing tone. 'The law courts would award it to you.'

'I don't want it. I didn't ask for it,' she gabbled. The wretched zipper had stuck. 'I didn't know my stepfather had gone to your family for money until he handed me the thousand dollars for...for...'

'Yes, that was very clever of him, handing over enough money to convince you it was meant for an abortion. Which, of course, neatly tied off the scam for him. No child. No more interest from the Peretti family. No comeback for him to worry about.'

Luc rolled off his interpretation of the situation so fast, Skye was distracted by how closely it matched her own anguished reasoning. She stopped struggling with the zipper to stare at him. 'You believe me?'

'Without a doubt,' he assured her.

Which instantly played havoc with her heart. If only he had believed her against his brother and those terrible photos...

'It's abundantly clear that your stepfather saw the opportunity to milk the situation for all he could get, intending to feather his own nest,' Luc went on, reminding Skye he was working off evidence this time, as well.

His belief in her word meant nothing!

Easy enough to deduce the truth from the investigator's report, which had supplied the date when her stepfather had left Sydney, flitting off to the Gold Coast in Queensland. It had also stated the money had been gambled away and her stepfather's current credit rating was not only nil, but criminal charges were pending over embezzlement at the used car yard where he'd worked as a salesman.

Her stepfather!

Skye burned over the rotten deception he'd played.

'At least he isn't my real father,' she flashed at Luc. 'I don't have to live with him like you do yours.'

Maurizio Peretti had also played a rotten deception, keeping the news of her pregnancy from Luc, intent on feathering his nest with the *right* kind of woman for his precious son.

Skye resumed tugging at the zipper, telling herself it was stupid to be affected by anything Luc said. He had probably moved on to relationships with women who were far more compatible with his family. Which would make his father's judgement ultimately right.

'My father has been made very aware of my feelings about his past actions on my behalf,' Luc answered grimly. 'He knows not to interfere between us again.'

'I just don't want him or you or anybody employed by your family to interfere with *me,*' Skye said fiercely, finally getting the zipper open, removing the cheque and thrusting it at Luc. 'Take back your blood money. It won't buy me or Matt.'

He shook his head, leaving the cheque hanging from her hand. 'It wasn't meant to buy you, Skye. It was meant to contribute what a father should, at least in financial support, towards his child's upbringing.'

'I've managed without it all these years and I much prefer to keep it that way.'

'It wasn't right that you had to manage alone,' he strongly demurred.

'Do you think this makes anything *right,* Luc?' she mocked savagely.

'It can help.'

'No. We occupy different worlds and Matt belongs in mine. It won't be good for him to have that line blurred by your money. I won't have it. Please…take it back.'

Again he shook his head.

Frustrated by his refusal and hating even the feel of the paper representing an obscene amount of money, she ripped it into pieces, marched over to a nearby litter bin and dropped the fragments into it, determined on making the point that he couldn't buy into his son's life.

'Money corrupts,' she flung at him as she wiped her hands of its touch. 'We both have firsthand knowledge of that, don't we, Luc?'

'It can, but it doesn't have to,' he argued. 'It can be used to good effect. Which was what it was meant for.'

Maybe…maybe not. Skye knew she wasn't prepared to risk finding out how good the intentions were behind so much money. She walked back from the litter bin, feeling lighter and more self-assured. 'I can manage without it,' she said with confidence. 'I've proved that already. Matt is a happy, well-adjusted little boy. He doesn't need—'

'You're not thinking of him,' Luc sliced in, an aggressive note of accusation warning her he was going on the attack now that she had destroyed the money link he'd tried to forge. No more soothing. 'You've made this choice because it's what *you* want,' he threw at her.

'I'm his mother,' she retorted, ramming home the close relationship he'd never had with their child. 'I know what's best for him.'

'Like my father knew what was best for me?' he shot back, bleak mockery in his eyes.

The challenge and the expression behind it gave Skye pause for thought. It was true she was reacting to her previous experience with the Peretti family, not wanting anything to do with them, not wanting Matt to have anything to do with them, either. But was she doing right by…their son?

Her gut feeling was *yes*.

Or was that fear talking—fear of becoming involved in something she might not be able to control.

Controlling the path of his son's life was what Maurizio Peretti had been about in breaking up her relationship with Luc. Was she heading the same way herself with Matt, making decisions for him she had no right to make?

'Can you honestly say, six years down the track, that your father didn't know what was best for you?' she asked.

'Yes, I can,' Luc replied without hesitation. His eyes bored into hers with searing intensity as he softly added, 'I lost you. And I lost five years of my son's life.'

The different tone, and the mountain of feeling behind it, shook Skye into protesting, 'But you must have met other women who were more…more compatible with your family.'

'Oh, yes.' His mouth curled cynically. 'I've had many *suitable* women paraded in front of me. Not one did I want to take as my wife.'

'Why not?'

'Because I couldn't feel with them what I'd felt with you, Skye.'

'That's gone,' she said defensively, frightened of him sensing her vulnerability to the strong attraction that *should* have died…but hadn't.

He didn't reply. He simply looked at her, making her skin crawl over the lie she had spoken. But she would not take it back, couldn't afford to take it back. How could she ever trust him again with her heart?

'Yes, what we once had is gone,' he finally agreed, the regret in his voice hitting her hard as he added, 'And the fault was mine in not believing your word against Roberto's. It's true we've occupied different worlds and that, too, was part of it. You might have come after me to pursue the truth if I'd been more accessible to you.'

No. She'd been too crushed to attempt a fighting pursuit. The memory of how he'd looked at her, how he'd spoken to her, how he'd rejected her so utterly…even now, everything within her cringed from it. And knowing his family was behind the deception had added immeasurably to her sense of absolute defeat. Luc was right about that.

He cocked his head consideringly. 'I wonder how you would have reacted, shown photos of your sister—if you had one—on top of a man who looked like me, a man who was wearing a distinctive watch which you'd given me, and had a very personal identification mark—a man your sister swore was me. Would you have believed my denial, Skye?'

It was difficult to think herself into the turn-around scenario but in fairness to him, she tried to focus on it. Would she have believed a denial, knowing how attractive he was—rich, handsome, any woman's dream? Would she have believed he was hers and hers alone, given a sister's sworn word—and photographic evidence—that he'd been intimate with her, too? Wouldn't her insecurities about his family background have whispered to her that he was arrogantly having fun with both sisters?

'The difference is... I would have fought the accusation, far beyond what you did,' Luc said quietly, a wry sadness in his eyes. 'Though I certainly don't blame you for not trying. The simple truth is I had the resources to fight and you didn't. Which was what my family counted on. You didn't have the power or the money to find the photographer or the woman who looked like you, to prove your innocence. So my family won. And we lost something very special. I lost most of all. What we had together...and my child.'

Regardless of the heat in the air around them, her skin broke out in goose-bumps...as though ghosts of what might have been were wafting over the graveyard of their love. The poignant sense of loss squeezed her heart unbearably. She wrenched her gaze from his and stared out at Botany Bay, fiercely telling herself this was all water under the bridge. They couldn't go back. They couldn't change anything. And what they once had *was* gone. They were different people now. Time and experience had moved them even further apart.

'Is it fair for you to insist I keep losing, Skye?' he appealed.

'You made a choice,' she cried, fighting not to be drawn into making emotional concessions. Steeling herself to maintain a shield around the vulnerability he could still touch, she swung her gaze back to his. 'Do you think I'm ever going to forget your choice, Luc?'

'No.' He heaved a rueful sigh. 'I was hoping you might understand it.'

'I do. I always did.'

'And possibly…forgive it?'

'That, too.'

'Then…?'

'It's an issue of trust. I don't want you or your family anywhere near my son. I don't trust any of you to be fair. If you'd been fair to me, Luc, you would have investigated Roberto's claims. You admit you had the resources to do so.'

'Yes, in hindsight, I wish I'd done that. It makes me even more conscious of the need to be fair now. What good purpose would it serve to alienate you…the only parent my son has known? And clearly loves.'

Her chin lifted in pride. 'Matt and I do have a very special closeness. Why can't you just leave us alone, Luc? You walked away from me. Walk away from him, too. Go and forget we even exist. We'll all be happier that way.'

'No.' His chin lifted in hard aggression and the sudden gleam of ruthlessness in his eyes sent a shiver down her spine. 'I will not remain the loser where he is concerned. I'll fight for visitation rights if I have to. I'll drag this whole business through the lawcourts if I have to, and I will spare no one along the way. I don't care what it takes. I will be part of my son's life.'

The waves of relentless purpose coming from him were warning enough that her worst fears could come true. Her chest felt so tight, it was as though Luc had just wrapped steel bands around it. No room to breathe. Nowhere to move.

'You can choose to make this a hostile battleground and put us all through hell,' he went on, making a flippant gesture towards the park bench. 'Or you can choose to sit down with me and discuss how Matt could benefit by having his father in his life.'

There was no choice and he knew it. The kind of fight he was threatening would be terribly damaging to Matt.

'What will it be, Skye?'

He was demanding a trust she couldn't give, but maybe he would earn it if he truly had Matt's best interests at heart.

'Of one thing you can be absolutely certain,' he said, mocking the turmoil of doubts in her mind. 'This time…this time…nothing on earth will make me walk away!'

CHAPTER FIVE

SATURDAY... Matt's first day with his father.

Luc instantly made the most of his arrival, turning up in a red Alfa hatchback, presenting Skye with the car keys and announcing, much to Matt's delight, that the car was for his Mummy, so she could drive him to soccer training during the week and matches on the weekend.

An expensive Italian car, not a cheap runaround which would have been far more suitable. The house they lived in did not have a garage attached. The car had to be left parked in the street and a red Alfa would stick out like a sore thumb in this neighbourhood. But did a Peretti think like that? No. And she hadn't thought to advise Luc sensibly when he'd insisted she needed her own transport for the activities *his son* would want to pursue.

Like soccer. Matt's friends at school were signing up for soccer today. Skye hadn't driven a car since her mother had died and the Alfa made her nervous, not to mention having Luc sitting beside her in the front passenger seat. Somehow she managed to get them to the football oval without doing anything stupid.

Luc took care of the signing up. Skye gritted her teeth over the pride in Matt's voice as he announced to his play-mates, 'This is my father.'

So far he'd been quite shy with Luc, wary of what

46

this new intrusion in his life might mean, not quite understanding the background and sensing Skye's fearful reservations. But even a little boy could see that the other boys' fathers did not match up to Luc Peretti, certainly not in looks, and not in authoritative and charismatic presence.

They were exchanging smiles now.

With a sinking heart, Skye realised there'd be no stopping an attachment forming. Luc was intent on it and Matt was responding.

He'd better not walk away, she thought fiercely. If he ever hurt Matt as he'd hurt her… Skye took a deep breath and unclenched her hands. It was impossible to fight this. All she could do was watch over it, which *she* had insisted upon. No way would she agree to Luc taking Matt anywhere without her, and nowhere that didn't have her approval. To her intense relief he had made those concessions.

For now, she added to herself.

She didn't trust him to keep to them for long.

Next stop was a shopping mall where Luc had Matt fitted with a proper pair of soccer boots, which he paid for. They proceeded to a toy shop where he also bought for Matt a soccer ball and a goal structure complete with netting so *his son* could practise shooting goals—which could have been done with simply setting up two sticks in the backyard.

Skye could feel herself bristling at the money being spent without a second thought. They ate lunch in a restaurant—another expensive exercise—with Matt full of excitement at being treated to his favourite chicken nuggets and a banana smoothie. He ate and drank with gusto, while Skye could barely swallow the chicken Caesar salad Luc had ordered for her, remembering it had been one of her favourite meals when they'd been going out together.

She didn't want those memories revived. It was hard enough, having to be with Luc all day, having to be agreeable for Matt's sake, feeling forced to accept the Peretti largesse which was bound to have an insidious influence on Matt.

At least the buying stopped with lunch. She drove them home and Luc spent the afternoon in the backyard with Matt, setting up the goal, showing how to kick the soccer ball with the side of the foot, not the toe, practising dribbling the ball and demonstrating other skills that fascinated Matt into trying to copy them.

It hurt to watch them—father and son—having fun together, chatting, laughing, cheering and clapping achievements. Matt was having a great time, completely relaxed now with his new Dad, liking him and loving the different kind of attention he was getting. *Male* attention. *Male* understanding. *Male* activity.

It brought home to Skye that no single parent could supply everything a child needed, no matter how well-balanced one tried to be. Better to have the input from both parents, *if* it could be given in harmony. And it had to be conceded Luc was delivering on his promises. So far.

At last the day was over, with Matt bathed, fed, put to bed and enjoying the novelty of reading his father a story before lights out. Luc was astonished that his five-year-old son could actually read, and when they left Matt's bedroom, having kissed him goodnight, Skye found herself being forcibly steered back to the kitchen instead of carrying out her intention to see Luc out the front door.

'Let go of me!' she growled, resenting being denied a ready escape from the prolonged tension of his company.

'I just want to say thank you, Skye,' he said reasonably, releasing her arm once he'd accomplished his purpose of regaining territorial advantage.

She stepped away quickly, moving to put the small kitchen table between them, instinctively rubbing at the heat he'd left on her skin. He frowned at the action but she'd didn't care if he found it offensive. He had no right to touch her, to use his dominant strength to get his own way.

'I don't want you frightened of me,' he said in sharp concern.

'Then please leave. You've had your day. You've said thank you. There's no reason for you to stay any longer.'

He shook his head, still frowning. 'Did I do something wrong with Matt?'

'No. He had a happy first day with you.'

He raised his hands in a gesture of appeal. 'So why can't we talk about it?'

'What do you want? My stamp of approval?' she snapped, screaming inside for him to go because any more of him today was unbearable. She'd had to hold in so much for Matt's sake, pretending she was pleased for him to have his father, giving Luc the freedom to court his son, while all the time feeling that the little world she had constructed was under terrible attack.

Instead of answering, Luc eyed her with searching

intensity, looking for the reason behind her hostile stance. 'Is it really so hard to share him with me, Skye?' he asked in the soft tone that stripped her of defences.

She gripped the back of a chair, trying to hold herself together. Tears were welling—tears of emotional exhaustion—and the lump in her throat made it difficult to speak. 'You've won him over,' she pushed out. 'It's done. Please…just go now. Let yourself out.'

Her eyes blurred and she swung blindly around, stepping over to the sink, frantically turning on the taps so as to look busy, though there was nothing to wash, only a glass that had already been rinsed. She didn't hear Luc move, didn't even sense him closing in on her. Her whole concentration was aimed at not breaking up before he went.

It shocked her when his hand reached out and turned off the taps. Her fingers didn't have the strength to resist when the glass was taken from them and placed on the draining rack. Her mind was completely seized up, incapable of directing any action. Her body could have been that of a rag doll's as Luc turned her towards him, wrapping her in a supportive embrace, holding her, pressing her head onto his shoulder, rubbing his cheek against her hair with a tenderness that broke open the floodgates to the tears she'd tried so hard to contain.

The storm of weeping was draining, reducing her to such a helpless state, she couldn't find the pride that might have dragged her away from him. His broad shoulder was there to lean on. His warmth and strength was like a blanket of comfort. And it had been a long, long time since anyone had held her, emitting a sense of caring.

That it was Luc didn't seem to matter. In fact, the familiarity of past intimacy between them somehow made it easy to sag against his body. It didn't feel strange or wrong. There was a sense of belonging that she simply didn't have the will to fight, however false it might be.

Eventually the tears dried up, leaving her aching from the emotional upheaval and limp from all the energy spent. She became conscious of Luc's fingers gently raking through her hair and realised he must have removed the clip at the back of her neck, releasing and loosening the long flow of it—a liberty—but she didn't mind. It felt good.

'Skye—' her name gravelled from his throat as though scraping over painful barriers '—I'm not trying to win Matt from you. Please believe that.'

She closed her eyes and dragged in a deep breath, needing to fill her lungs with air, ease the ache in her chest. She felt too tired to speak. Her mind didn't want to take up the fight over trust. It was too hard.

'You're his mother,' Luc went on, a deeper, strong throb in his voice—a throb that somehow moved into her sluggish bloodstream and revived all the maternal feelings in her heart.

'You've done a wonderful job of bringing up our son. You can be very proud of the boy he is…the boy you've shaped him to be…'

The warmth of his approval flooded through her.

'I don't know how to thank you…doing it all alone. He's amazing. A happy child, well-mannered, eager to have a go at everything, and reading at his young age…'

He sounded so awed, a smile tugged at the corners of Skye's mouth. She was proud of Matt. Justly proud. And she was glad Luc felt she had done a good job of bringing up their son.

'If you've been thinking I might take him away from you, I swear to you I won't, Skye. That was never my intention. And seeing how he is to-day…why would I want to? Matt couldn't have a better mother. So please…don't be afraid of me.'

She didn't want to be. But even if he truly meant what he said now…she stirred herself to raise her head, open her eyes, look straight at him, speak her fears. 'Today…Matt was a novelty to you and you were a novelty to Matt. It won't stay that way. You won't want to give him so much quality time and if Matt feels let down by you…'

'I'll do my best not to let him down.'

'Things change, Luc. Other people can interfere…'

'Not this time.' The resolute gleam in his eyes suddenly burned into something else entirely. 'And some things don't change.'

Her heart kicked in alarm as he whipped his hands up to cup her face, his thumbs slowly fanning the line of her lower lip, making it tingle. 'Remember how it was, Skye?'

Raw desire was blazing at her, furring his voice, stunning her into mesmerised passivity. Her hands were pressed against his chest but she didn't think to push away. Some magnetic force kept them glued there. She didn't think to move her head aside, either, though his was bending closer and closer, his intention unmistakable. She was conscious only of a thundering need to let it happen…to know, to feel, to match the memory.

His mouth covered hers, instantly triggering an electric sensitivity. She hadn't been kissed since he had last kissed her and her mind filled with wonder that it could be so fascinating, so seductive, the soft sensuality of having her lips tasted, the exciting slick of his tongue opening them further, teasing and tantalising as it slid into her mouth to entice hers into play.

The temptation to respond was irresistible. The desire to feel again what she'd once felt with him surged out of the sense of having been cheated of it, cut off as though she was dead, through no fault of her own.

But she wasn't dead. It was as if every cell in her body was springing into vibrant life, screaming out for what had been lost. She wanted it back—the all-consuming passion they'd shared. He owed it to her. He owed her so much…

A torrent of feelings pumped through her, driving her out of passivity, long-buried needs rising, demanding at least some satisfaction. Her tongue sprang into an erotic tango with his. Her hands clawed their way up his chest, over his shoulders, fingers thrusting through the thick matt of his hair, curling around his head, fiercely denying any end to the kiss which turned into a wild battleground for possession—invasion, assault, frenzied passion, no retreat, ragged pauses only to regather breath enough to engage again.

He no longer held her face. His hands clutched her bottom, fingers digging into the soft rounded flesh as he dragged her closer, lifting her into more intimate contact with him, and a mad exultation fizzed through her brain as she felt his arousal. She rubbed against it, wantonly provocative, deliberately stirring the desire he'd turned his back on, building the heat he had doused with ice, not believing it had only been for him.

No ice now.

He wrenched his mouth from hers, scooped her off her feet, and carried her out of the kitchen, down the central hallway, into her bedroom at the front of the house, his chest heaving but there was not one falter in the long, strong strides that were driven by the compulsion to get her to a bed.

Skye didn't protest, didn't struggle to assert herself in any way. It was wildly exhilarating to be swept off by Luc, knowing he wasn't thinking of anything but having her—the woman he'd cast out of his life. He wasn't about to walk away now. Oh, no! And Skye's whole body tingled with a sense of power—a deep, primitive power that clamoured to be used, claiming this man as hers, so completely hers all the more *suitable* women would never get a chance with him.

It was twilight outside, almost dark in the bedroom, though she could see Luc clearly enough, see the strained look on his face as he put her down and worked at speed to strip them both. No finesse in the undressing. No stopping to touch, kiss or caress. Urgent need.

She didn't try to help or hinder, didn't care about her own nakedness. She watched him, secretly revelling in the desire that couldn't wait, that was raging out of Luc's control, his eyes hungrily feasting on her femininity as he moved onto the bed, knees intent on parting her legs, his own magnificent physique right in her face now, smooth shiny olive skin stretched over tight muscles, his whole body yearning for hers, craving the union he'd put behind him.

And for a moment she hated him for it, a fierce flash of hatred for the contempt he'd dealt out, making all she'd given of herself negligible, dirty...yet everything within her sighed a sweet welcome as he entered her, plunging deep, filling the emptiness she'd known for far too long.

He paused there, sighing himself, and Skye savagely hoped it signalled the feeling of having come home—home to where his heart was. Except she couldn't really believe it because he would never have left her if that was true.

She closed her eyes and focused on feeling him inside her, no longer caring what it meant for him, wanting to recapture all the sensations she had forgotten, the rippling pleasures of the rhythm, the build-up of intense physical excitement. And Luc delivered. He always had delivered. Not usually as roughly as this. But that had its exciting edge, too, knowing control had been sabotaged by need, adding to the power of his wanting her.

He was breathing hard.

She was, too, her body instinctively accommodating the wild pounding, exulting in it, her legs wound around his taut buttocks urging him on, her back arched, her hands raking the bunched muscles of his shoulders, the tips of her breasts brushing his chest as he rocked back and forth in a frenzy of driven possession, the tension of it becoming more and more explosive.

The shattering started, the ecstatic meltdown she had only ever known with him, and even as she started floating with it, she felt the release of his climax, the jerking spurts of heat spilling from him, mingling with her own contentment, increasing the sweet pleasure of it, the sense of fulfilment that matched the memories.

He collapsed on top of her, his face buried in the stream of her hair across the pillow, and she hugged him tightly to her, clutching the intimacy of the moment before it went away. For this little time, at least, he was hers, and she consciously shut out the realities of the worlds they occupied, feeling only their togetherness—a dream that had been lost—a dream that couldn't last.

CHAPTER SIX

HER beautiful hair, soft, silky, incredibly sensual…the feel of it, the feel of her, had started this, propelling him down a path he hadn't meant to take yet, and certainly not with the frenzied need that had driven his every action. He had to start thinking now, seize advantage of the knowledge that the need had been mutual.

She was clasping him tightly to her. Was it reaction to the physical upheaval of climaxing, or a desire to hold onto him? He had to move, take his weight off her before she became too conscious of it, too conscious of what she had allowed to happen, regretting it, spurning him as he'd once spurned her.

He rolled onto his back, carrying her with him, keeping one of her legs trapped by his to retain an intimate entanglement, using his hands to travel up and down the curve of her spine, over the soft roundness of her bottom, wanting her to feel him loving her, everything about her.

The sex had been too crude, too fast. He'd meant to woo her, win back her trust. Her fear of him had been intolerable, a barrier he'd had to break, though he'd lost sight of that aim as her tension had collapsed into tears. Holding her in his arms again—impossible not to remember how it had once been with her, stirring the urge to make her remember, too.

Show her, kiss her…

He hadn't anticipated the fierce response.

Given Skye's hostility—justified hostility—what was behind *her* burst of passion? He couldn't believe it was a raging desire for him. Though there was no doubting she had wanted the sexual connection, responding to it all the way. That certainly hadn't changed. But was it enough to build on?

It had to be because there was no going back to a more careful courtship. Besides, it would be better for Matt to have both parents as a constant in his life. And it would prove his own commitment to fatherhood to Skye, removing her fear of a transient and possibly damaging dalliance with his son. So best that he speak now, before her mind got active against him again.

Her head was resting over his heart. He wound a long tress of her hair around his hand to hold her there. He told himself she could not be more vulnerable to the idea than she was at this moment with both of them naked and intimately entwined, reinforcing what they could and did share.

It would come out baldly, he knew, but dressing it up with feelings she might scorn could very well tip the scales in a very negative fashion. She wouldn't trust emotions. Working from her reaction seemed the most viable option. He had to use reason and do it convincingly.

Trying to keep the enormous tension he felt out of his voice, Luc simply announced what he was aiming for.

'I want you to marry me.'

*   *   *

Marry him…

The shock of the proposal rolled through Skye's sluggish mind, setting off alarm signals. She hadn't wanted to think of what she'd done with Luc. Much easier to just drift in a haze of feeling, blocking re-alities out until they had to be faced. But a proposal of *marriage*…it was so off the wall, Skye struggled to get her head around what it meant.

She started to shift, acutely aware of his heart drumming under her ear—a soothing sound just a few moments ago—a disturbing one now.

'No. Stay with me.'

The brusque command unsettled her further. He had no right to force her compliance to his will, not over anything so personal as this. She'd conceded his right to involve himself with Matt, but what happened between her and Luc was most certainly a matter of choice. Just because she'd had sex with him didn't mean he could do anything he liked with her.

'Don't make this a fight, Luc,' she warned, trying to gather wits enough to understand what had moti-vated his proposal. 'Let me move.'

'Why do you want to?'

'I've just remembered who you are,' she an-swered, not caring if it hurt him, instinctively using shock to give herself room for retreat to a less vul-nerable position so she could think straight, not be influenced by the strong sexual connection he was pressing.

'Don't give me that!' He whipped her over onto her back and propped himself up, one arm on either side of her so that she was looking directly into his eyes—eyes blazing with a certainty that poured into passionate words. 'You knew who was kissing you… knew who brought you to this bed…knew who was—'

'Screwing me again?' she fired at him, angered by the physical domination he was exerting when she had made a clear request to be released.

His face tightened, his mouth compressing into a thin line. 'You wanted this, too, Skye,' he bit out, shaking his head over her accusation.

He was using it against her—the far too short-sighted surrender to what had probably always been a fantasy—her and Luc together, their love so strong it could ride through anything. It hadn't. And he'd moved on to other women while she had struggled on by herself. He'd still be moving on, but for Matt.

'Was it good for you, Luc?' she asked, resenting all his infidelities.

'Yes. And you wouldn't have responded as you did if it wasn't good for you,' he retorted, determined on making her admit it.

'So you think you can capitalise on it, move straight in and take over my life.'

'We're good together. We always were,' he argued.

'A pity you didn't remember that when it counted.'

'It counts now,' he snapped back, ignoring the past, accentuating the present. 'We have a son. We should be a family.'

Matt. She was right about what Luc really wanted. 'There's more to marriage than having a child. I don't want you as my husband.'

'You came to bed with me.'

She couldn't leave him with that weapon to use against her. 'I wanted you to remember what you gave up, Luc,' she said mockingly.

His brows beetled down into a deep frown.

'How many women have there been since me?' she asked, hating him for moving on, leaving her behind, then thinking he could turn around and take her as his wife when it suited him.

'They're irrelevant.' It was a fierce mutter, wanting her to forget them.

'When you shared a bed with them, did you remember me?'

'Yes, I did. Nothing was ever like what we had together.'

For a moment, his vehement reply rocked Skye out of her bitter train of thought. There had only ever been Luc for her. No one else. If he felt the same way... But he couldn't. He'd put his brother's word ahead of hers, his family's view of her ahead of his own.

'I don't believe you!' she cried, and with all her strength, slammed her hands against his shoulders and thrust him far enough away for her to scramble off the bed, out of reach.

'It's true!' he hurled after her.

'Be quiet! Matt's in the next room,' she hissed at him as she grabbed her houserobe from the one chair in her bedroom, putting it on as fast as she could, determined on shutting out any resumption of intimacy with him.

'Our son, Skye,' he swiftly reminded her, his voice lowered but still emphatic in delivery. 'Don't you think it would be better for him to have a full-time father as well as mother?'

She wrapped the robe around her and tied the belt savagely as she swung to face him again. 'That's what you're after, isn't it? Matt. Not me. Get the mother, get the boy.'

'Wrong! I want both of you.'

He was still stretched out on the bed, propped up on one arm, looking moody and magnificent, every part of him male perfection. No wonder she hadn't wanted any other man. And maybe never would. Which gave her pause for thought. She could have him. All she had to do was say yes to his marriage proposal.

But could she live with him—live with his family—and be happy? How could she trust any of them to really care about her, given how they'd treated her in the past?

She had to finish this—get him out of her bedroom, out of her house—not let him play on the desires he could so easily tap into. Treacherous feelings! The sense of intimacy still swirling in this darkened room drove her over to the light-switch by the door. She flicked it on, telling herself she would see more clearly now, think more clearly.

But it didn't help. Luc's nakedness gathered even more power in the light, vividly reminding her of how every part of him had felt. And his claim of wanting her burned from his eyes, heating her skin all over again, making her toes curl, making her stomach contract, making her breasts ache, her nipples tighten into tell-tale prominence.

Panicking over his effect on her, she folded her arms across the wildly fluttering beat of her heart and rushed into defensive speech. 'Don't think having sex with you means anything, Luc.'

'You can't make me believe you'd have sex indiscriminately, Skye.' His mouth curled in bitter irony. 'I believed it once and made the biggest mistake of my life. No one can sell it to me a second time.'

'This is different,' she hotly argued.

'How is it different?' he mocked.

She frantically sought a convincing explanation. 'Being pregnant hardly makes you desirable to other men. And having a baby takes up all your time, not to mention nursing your mother through chemotherapy, losing her, then trying to establish a life while being a single parent. I haven't had sex since I was with you six years ago and you caught me at a weak moment. That's all it was.'

'Because it *was* me,' he pointed out with arrogant certainty.

She glared at him, unable to deny a truth which was only too self-evident, anyway.

He stretched out an inviting arm. 'Come back to bed. Let me show you...'

'No!' The physical pleasure she knew he would give could not be allowed to cloud her mind again. 'I want you to get dressed and go, Luc.'

'Let me answer your needs, Skye,' he promised temptingly.

'You can't answer all of them,' she retorted. 'And please do as I ask. This wasn't in our agreement. If you have any integrity at all...'

He moved, swinging his legs off the bed. Fear of him coming at her choked off any further speech and drove her into instant recoil. She shrank back against the doorjamb, hugging herself even more tightly.

Luc sat on the edge of the bed, absolutely still, frowning at her. Every nerve in her body screeched with tension as she waited for his next action. The silence was electric with barely contained emotions and challenges she was too frightened to acknowledge, yet the strong sense of them pinned her to the wall, draining her of any further initiative.

'Integrity…' The word fell from his lips, heavy with guilt and regret. 'I lost faith in yours so you have no belief in mine.' He lifted deeply pained eyes, probing her soul with searing intensity. 'Did it ever occur to you that I cared too much about integrity, Skye? That seeing you…in bed with my brother…was such a killing blow…'

'I was never in bed with your brother!'

'Goddammit!' He rose to his feet, towering up to his full height, pumping out waves of violent energy as he hurled out his truth. 'It wasn't just the photos! You were charmed with Roberto's wit and you didn't stop him from flirting with you. Every time the three of us were together, Roberto would claim your attention and you gave it to him. Willingly!'

'He was nice to me, Luc. Your parents looked at me as though I was trash, treated me with icy politeness. Why wouldn't I warm to your brother?' she flung back at him.

'Warm…' His hands lifted, fingers outstretched like upturned talons, left empty and frustrated because what he'd wanted to hold on to had been ripped away. 'Where does warmth turn into heat? Roberto swore it was so…swore I was making a fool of myself for loving you…and there were the photos to prove it, to prove there was no integrity in your love for me…'

'It wasn't true,' Skye cried, deeply agitated by the

pain pouring from him and the artful lies that had been woven around her behaviour.

'He was my brother! We'd shared all our lives together! Why would he confess to such a divisive and destructive truth if it wasn't the truth?'

A killing blow...she could see it now, feel how it was for him.

'You were the light of my life and he tore it out of me and left me in darkness. A darkness so black I couldn't see you any more. Not the person you were.' His hands dropped in a helpless fashion as the raw anguish on his face fell into a terrible bleakness. 'All in the name of integrity...which he sacrificed...to please my father.'

He shook his head and slowly bent down to pick up his clothes as though there was nothing left to do and there was certainly no joy to be had from any more exposure. On any level.

A poignant sense of loss permeated the sudden silence and Skye's heart felt as though it was being wrung by merciless hands. The hurt was too great— his hurt and hers—what had been done to both of them! Her mind was a chaos of confusion. Was it wrong of her to keep blaming him for turning traitor to their love when he had suffered the devastation of a double treachery? The woman he loved...the brother he loved...

'Don't be frightened of me, Skye,' he said softly, looking at her with an expression of rueful appeal. He was putting on his shirt, doing up the buttons. 'This time around...it's not about taking from you. It's about giving.'

She couldn't bring herself to speak. She wasn't so

sure of her ground any more. All she could think of was how much she had loved this man and maybe she could love him again if…but weren't there too many *ifs?* And Matt was in the middle of them. Her precious son whom she had to protect against the Peretti family. She mustn't forget Matt, just because Luc could still get to her, twisting her around, making her feel…

Watching him pull on his underpants and jeans, everything within her quivered, not from fear but from the freshly awakened sexual memory of how it had been with him…the intimacy they'd shared on the very bed she had to sleep in tonight. Alone…as she'd been alone all these years. She had Matt but a child's love—her love for him—was different. Being a mother did not fulfil everything she wanted as a woman.

Luc tucked his shirt in, did up his zipper, shot her a look that mocked the security she'd wanted from him being clothed again. 'It won't go away—the chemistry between us, Skye. No matter what you're telling yourself, it will still be there next week, next month, next year, and all the years to follow.'

The relentless beat of his prediction struck chords of truth that twanged through her entire body. Her mind could produce no answer to it. She simply stared back at him, silently demanding the distance she needed right now, telling herself not to concede anything more at this point.

He sat on the bed to put on his socks and Reeboks, doing it with commendable alacrity, not dragging out his time with her. He stood up and she stiffened her backbone, determined on an air of self-containment as he walked over to the doorway, emanating a dynamic energy that would not acknowledge defeat.

He paused beside her, his dark brilliant eyes engaging hers in an intense battle of wills. 'I can't give you back the years that were taken from us but we can make a future together,' he said quietly.

They had to…around Matt. But she now knew Luc was intent on pushing for more, and even as she thought it, he laid it out to her again.

'I doubt any marriage is perfect, but I promise you this. I'll work damned hard at making it as good as I can for you. Think about it, Skye. I'll be back next Saturday…as agreed.'

He walked on into the hallway. She heard the front door click open, then shut behind him.

Gone.

Air whooshed out of her lungs on a huge sigh of relief. She sagged against the wall, staring at the bed where she had wantonly surrendered her independence. Was it possible to claw it back? Did she want to? Did she have to?

She needed to know the answers before Luc came again.

Next Saturday.

As agreed.

Because he was Matt's father.

CHAPTER SEVEN

'DADDY'S here!' Matt yelled from the front porch. 'And he's come in *his* red car!'

The Ferrari! The excitement in her son's voice shot Skye out of dallying in the kitchen. He'd been outside, waiting and watching for his father in a fever of impatience, and the double attraction of the Ferrari spelled danger! She raced down the hallway to the opened front door in time to see Matt unlatching the gate and Luc emerging from his car on the other side of the street.

'Don't run onto the road, Matt!' she called.

It alerted Luc, who instantly spotted him and held up a hand. 'Wait on the sidewalk.' Commanding authority.

Matt obeyed, but he literally jiggled with pleasure as Luc strode across the road towards him, smiling his own pleasure in this obvious welcome from his son. He swooped down, picked him up and hoisted him up against his shoulder, laughing as Matt laughed—the sound of mutual happiness. 'So how did it go at soccer training?' he asked.

And Matt bubbled over with news of the two after-school sessions he'd attended during the week. No shyness. A quick and easy rapport with his father, plus unadulterated delight in his interest and company.

Which put a little hollow in Skye's heart. It was

hard, realising she couldn't supply all her son's needs. Not even years of loving him, doing everything she could for him, was enough. He wanted his father.

She waited on the porch, watching them bonding as Luc carried Matt back to her. They *were* alike, though maybe she was seeing the similarities more acutely now that it was impossible to deny them with Luc right in front of her again. And he wasn't going to go away.

The only question was…how far should she let him into their lives?

All week she had been weighing it up in her mind and was no closer to an answer. It was no use even trying to think of him as the much younger Luc she had loved. He was different, just as she was different. He'd spoken of darkness and she sensed it ran very deeply, married to a steely resolve that encompassed her because of what had been done to him.

She wasn't sure love had any part in it…yet watching him with Matt, seeing him drink in the innocence of his child's natural response to him…his heart was surely being touched. It wasn't just ownership.

So maybe he was still capable of loving. Whether that could extend to her…if she was his wife…but there was still the Peretti family in the background, a powerful father who would hate having his will thwarted.

Then Luc turned his gaze from Matt to her, a direct blaze of power that thumped into her heart and burned into her brain the unequivocal fact that he wasn't about to have his will thwarted, either.

'Daddy said I had to ask you if I can have a ride in his car,' Matt piped up. 'Can I, Mummy? Can I?'

'May I,' Skye corrected automatically, wrenching her gaze away from Luc's, 'We can't all fit in that car, Matt. If we're going to Darling Harbour…' The outing agreed upon.

'Perhaps a quick spin around the block?' Luc suggested.

'He's not a stranger any more, Mummy. It can't be a bad thing to do.'

Skye flushed at the reminder of the argument she'd used in a protective need to keep Luc a stranger to Matt. 'Just a short ride then,' she muttered, feeling hamstrung by her own dictate.

'Five minutes at most,' Luc promised, undoubtedly realising it was stretching her trust to let him go off alone with their son. It was against their agreement.

'Okay, five minutes,' she conceded, shooting him a warning look. One transgression didn't mean he could trample anywhere he liked.

He grinned at her, triumph dancing in his eyes. Matt whooped with joy and they were off, leaving Skye to fret over the feeling that control was slipping away from her.

In fact, it had been slipping away ever since Luc had re-entered her life. Her independent stance was gone. Any peace of mind was gone. The future directions she had been considering were hopelessly blurred by the now prime consideration of whether or not she should entertain the idea of marrying Luc Peretti.

With a helpless sigh, Skye retreated into the house, checked that everything needed for their day out had been put in the backpack before zipping it shut, slung it over one arm, grabbed both her hat and Matt's, and went back out to the porch, locking the front door behind her.

The Ferrari came vrooming down the street as she walked towards the Alfa. Luc had kept his word. He didn't want her to be frightened of him. The problem was it was difficult not to be when her knees went weak at the sight of him.

She unlocked the Alfa and waited beside it, wondering how she was going to cope in his company all day long—a morning visit to the aquarium, lunch in one of the many restaurants overlooking Darling Harbour, idling the afternoon away at the children's playground or the Japanese Gardens.

Father and son emerged from the Ferrari, holding hands to cross the road, both of them wearing jeans and T-shirts, just as she was. The three of them were dressed like a family, going on a holiday tour together, and Matt was skipping with excited anticipation. He'd had his ride in his father's flash car and now he was going to see all the fish from his favourite movie, *Finding Nemo.*

Skye handed the Alfa's key to Luc. 'You drive. I haven't been near inner-city traffic for so long, it would make me nervous.'

'Then this should be a practice run for you,' he argued.

'I'd rather do that alone.'

'I could help you avoid mistakes.'

'Just let me be a passenger, Luc. It's your day with Matt.' *Not with me.*

He instantly picked up the implication not to assume too much and gave her an ironic little smile as he took the key. 'Keeping your distance, Skye?'

'Keeping out of trouble,' she answered.

She had trouble enough, sitting so closely beside him in the car on their way to Darling Harbour. His physical presence in such a small space dominated her consciousness, even though she kept her gaze fixed on the traffic, trying her utmost to ignore how acutely all her other senses were attuned to him.

Nor could she stop her body from feeling all keyed up—whether to repel any touch from him or welcome it, she didn't know. Just being near him aroused the fresh sexual memories from last week, but she couldn't let that happen again, couldn't risk any kind of intimate contact while she was still trying to sort through the situation between them.

Matt was full of chatter, keeping Luc engaged in conversation, for which Skye was intensely grateful. She listened to their voices. No strain in either of them—happy, cheerful, having fun. Would Luc be a good father in the long run? Discovering a son was still very new to him. He wanted to indulge Matt, but there was more to parenting than indulgence.

Still, Skye couldn't quarrel with the indulgence when they finally reached the aquarium and walked into a new entrancing world for Matt. The touching pond and the showcases of fish were fantastic. Seeing sharks swimming overhead was positively awesome. She could not have afforded to give Matt this experience and he was loving every minute of it.

The tropical fish, of course, were a very special attraction, and he told Luc the names of those he recognised from having watched *Finding Nemo* many times since Skye had bought him the video for Christmas. Naturally the clownfish was his favourite.

Eventually they'd exhausted every attraction and Skye suggested a toilet visit before going on to lunch. She automatically took Matt's hand to lead him into the Ladies' Room, only to be halted by Luc.

'He should come with me, Skye.'

'But he's a little boy,' she objected.

'I'll look after him.' Hard challenge in his eyes.

It was *his* day with Matt.

Rather than make a fight of it, Skye reluctantly let them go together. She was waiting for them when they came out and Matt rushed over to her to whisper proudly, 'I peed in the urinal with Daddy.'

Skye grimaced over this highly basic piece of male bonding and rolled her eyes at Luc who was totally unabashed about it. 'About time I had a first in my son's upbringing,' he said pointedly, reminding her of all the *firsts* he'd missed—first word, first step, first day at school…

Matt skipped on ahead of them as they walked towards the aquarium exit and Luc seized the chance for some private talk between them, stunning her with his opening line. 'Any chance you might have conceived another child last week?'

'No,' she answered quickly, a wave of heat whooshing up her neck at the abrupt reference to their intimacy.

'I didn't use protection, Skye, and your own long drought from any sex suggests you didn't, either.'

'It was a safe time.' A fact she'd only figured out— frantically—when the possible consequence of pregnancy had occurred to her after he'd gone.

'Sure about that?'

'Yes,' she bit out grimly, remembering the churning panic while she had checked dates.

'I was rather hoping it wasn't,' he drawled.

'What?' She threw an appalled look at him.

'I'm here to take care of you this time.' His eyes glittered ruthless determination. 'And I'd like us to have a child we both shared from the very beginning.'

She felt his strongly embittered sense of having been cheated of years with Matt and kept her mouth shut. This was not something she could argue against. Yet a revulsion against the ruthlessness she saw in him forced her to ask, 'Were you thinking of getting me pregnant when you carried me off to bed?'

'No.' He sliced her a sardonic little smile. 'I just wanted you, Skye. So much that protection didn't enter my head. And it didn't enter yours, either.' He paused before softly adding, 'What do you think that says about our need for each other?'

She didn't answer.

Luc called out to Matt, bringing him back in line with them, taking his hand—a hand that was readily given, unlike hers. Skye wondered if Luc would stoop to seriously playing Matt as a persuasive force in getting her to accept his proposal of marriage. Or was he simply counting on her own vulnerability to a connection with him?

She couldn't block out the powerful attraction he exerted on her, yet marriage was something else entirely. No way was she going to rush into a decision. Six years was a huge gap to bridge and she was far too conscious of the murky waters that flowed all around them, making a foundation on which to build seem very rocky.

They proceeded to a harbourside restaurant where Luc had booked a table out on the open terrace so they could watch the colourful passing parade of people and the boats in the water—lots of boats on show this weekend, reminding Skye of how she had first met Luc and his brother.

It was at the end of her second year of university and she'd got a casual summer job in the supply shop at the big Cronulla marina. The Peretti family had owned a huge waterfront home nearby in those days. Probably still did. She and her mother had moved from the adjoining suburb of Caringbah after her stepfather had deserted them.

But that summer, the Peretti brothers had sailed every weekend. She had met Roberto first, serving him in the shop. He'd flirted with her and she'd thought him a rather gorgeous playboy until Luc had appeared, completely knocking out the attraction of his younger brother. It wasn't so much he was better looking, more that he somehow made Roberto seem lightweight in comparison, instantly relegated to the sidelines.

He still had that power.

Skye glanced around the men seated at other tables, the men walking by…all of them paled in comparison to Luc. He commanded attention, compelled attention, and she knew she was in a hopeless position, trying to hold him at a distance when he was intent on reclaiming her.

After lunch they strolled down to the playground area where Luc directed that he and Skye sit on a grassy bank, watching how brave Matt was at using the slippery dip by himself. Encouraged to show off,

Matt was only too eager to demonstrate to his father how capable he was of using all the playground equipment, which neatly took him out of earshot.

Skye resigned herself to another private conversation with Luc, knowing there was no ultimate way of avoiding it. One way or another, he'd make the opportunity. Besides, her nerves were so on edge waiting for it, she might as well get it over with. They sat side by side, their knees hitched up, arms resting on them, no doubt looking very relaxed together to Matt, and at least Luc made no move to get closer.

'Let's discuss marriage,' he started without any preamble.

Skye plucked a blade of grass and began slowly shredding it as she struggled to put her thoughts into some kind of sensible framework.

'You've had time to think about it,' Luc pressed.

'I don't know the man you are now,' Skye said truthfully, keeping her focus on the strips of grass.

'You want more time.'

'Yes.'

'Then you *are* considering it.'

The satisfaction in his voice stirred rebellion against the pressure he was laying on her. 'There's a hell of a lot to consider, Luc.'

He came straight back with, 'Tell me what's on your mind.'

More pressure.

She slanted him a curious look. 'Have you run the idea of marrying me past your parents, Luc?'

'I didn't discuss it with them, no. I told them flatly that they either accept you as my wife or lose me.

And having just lost one son, I don't think they'll be inclined to buck my ultimatum.'

It shocked her speechless. She stared at him, stunned by the starkly drawn stand he had made, the sheer ruthlessness of his planning, and the assumption that they would marry, all laid out as though it was already decided.

'When…' Her mouth had gone so dry she had to work some moisture in it before managing to choke out the question skating through her dazed mind. 'When did you tell them?'

'After I faced my father with your accusation that he'd paid for an abortion,' he said matter-of-factly. 'And the whole truth of what had happened six years ago was finally disclosed.'

Not this past week…much, much before…after coming face to face with her and Matt for the first time. He'd decided *then!* Was it to spite his father for keeping all knowledge of Matt from him—a vengeful act on his whole family for having sabotaged his right to choose whatever woman he wanted in his life?

'Your parents won't want me as your wife,' she stated with utter certainty.

A hard relentless pride looked back at her. 'They don't have a choice.'

'I do, Luc,' she pointedly reminded him.

'They will accept you, Skye. They have too much to lose if they don't.'

'I don't want to be involved in your fight with them. I don't want Matt to be a pawn in your game. He'll feel it. He'll know he's not what they want. You can't force approval from people when they don't feel it inside.'

'This is no game, Skye. Believe me, I'm deadly serious.'

Deadly was right, she thought.

'My parents will love Matt. Unreservedly,' he pushed on, laying out cogent arguments. 'He's their only grandchild and the only one they'll have if you don't marry me. Roberto is dead and his marriage produced no children. The whole future of the Peretti family is now narrowed down to *our* son.' His smile held a dark wealth of satisfaction as he added, 'That makes Matt very precious to them.'

A convulsive little shiver ran down Skye's spine. 'Don't put that weight on me. Or Matt,' she cried. 'It's not fair!'

'I think it balances the scales very nicely. You should feel it does, too, Skye.'

She shook her head. 'You're taking advantage of your brother's death. For all the wrong he did to me and to you, it doesn't make this right. Nothing can make this right.' It was incredibly painful to say it but she truly felt the alternative would cause even more pain. 'You should marry someone else...leave Matt and me out of it.'

'But I won't, Skye.' In a soft, insidiously invasive voice that curled around her heart, demanding entry, he added, 'You're the only woman I've ever loved...or will love.'

She jerked her head away, frightened of showing how deeply it touched her when she hadn't realised herself how much it would mean.

He must have interpreted it as a negative reaction. With barely a pause he spoke in a much harder tone, determined possession underlining every word.

'And Matt is my son.'

CHAPTER EIGHT

'THEY'RE grading all the kids for the soccer teams tomorrow,' Matt announced on the way home from Darling Harbour. 'Can you come, Daddy?'

'Your father has other things to do tomorrow,' Skye quickly inserted, panicking at the thought of having to withstand Luc's pursuit of marriage with her a second day in a row. Besides, a Sunday visit was not part of their agreement. Her hands clenched, the need to fight against any pressure racing through her mind.

'I bet all the other fathers will be there,' Matt grumbled.

Luc's hands tightened around the steering wheel. Skye's heart sank. She knew what Luc was thinking—robbed of five years of fatherhood and still being blocked from taking part in his son's life. It violated *his* sense of justice and threw Skye into confusion over what was fair and what wasn't.

Was she being selfish, limiting his access to Matt? Did she have to protect them both from the Peretti family when Luc had placed himself so unequivocally beside them, prepared to ward off any harmful interference in their lives?

'It's not until four o'clock,' Matt informed, his voice brightening with the hope the late time might make a difference. 'You can have all day to do other things.'

Skye closed her eyes despairingly. It wasn't Luc using Matt to pressure her into doing what *he* wanted. Their son was doing a good job of it all by himself. She heard Luc's swift intake of breath hissing between his teeth. He was hating this, and God help her, she hated it, too. It wasn't how it should be for Matt.

Luc spoke, determinedly testing her resistance to the idea. 'Perhaps I could come by the soccer park...'

Words left hanging for her to pick up on, words carefully strained of any forceful persuasion, words that begged this concession from her.

And she heard herself say, 'Matt would like that.'

Luc's relief was palpable.

The thin edge of the wedge, Skye thought, but it was difficult to regret it, listening to Matt's bubbling pleasure in the possibility his father would come to watch him.

Not possibility.

Certainty.

Skye had no doubt about that. Luc confirmed it before he left that evening, pausing on the front porch to thank her for stretching their agreement and thankfully not pressing her for anything else.

Though his eyes did. His eyes bored into hers, intent on smashing every barrier between them. She knew he wouldn't be content until there were no limitations on their relationship. But she wasn't sure what was the driving force behind the burning intent.

Love...possession...revenge?

All of them powerful feelings.

Long into the night Skye lay awake, feeling her own way through Luc's current conflict with his parents. He'd thrown down the gauntlet to them—lose him or accept her as his wife and Matt as his son. He expected to win the challenge, but would he?

The method used to separate them last time had been an extreme act, demonstrating the depth of his family's opposition to a relationship which didn't fit into their world. To Skye's mind, their grief over losing their younger son, was highly unlikely to change their attitude towards her. They would want Luc to fulfil their plans for him even more now—their one son left to uphold all they stood for.

Luc thought Matt would be a swaying factor—their one grandchild—but Skye doubted *her* son had the power to pull them into acceptance. The trust fund proved how much they would pay to keep the unwanted by-blow out of their lives. He wasn't wanted any more than she was.

They probably saw Luc's reaction to Roberto's deathbed confession as a rebellion against having been manipulated into giving up a woman he'd wanted—shock at discovering he had a child. His knowledge might stay their hand from any further interference with her life or Matt's, but there would surely be mounting pressure on Luc to drop them from his life.

It could become a very bitter battle.

Luc had spoken of his parents losing but Skye couldn't see them rolling over to oblige what might be considered as only wounded pride on his part. Yet it wasn't pride she felt pulsing from him when he was with her and Matt. It was need. And it kept stirring need in her, as well. Even more unsettling...need in Matt.

Where would it all end?

Roberto's deathbed revelations had set in motion a train of action she had no way of stopping. Luc was the engine driver and she and Matt were captive passengers. All she could hope for was they didn't crash against an immovable force which would break them apart with worse wounds to carry into the future.

Eventually Skye fell into a fretful sleep. She was wakened the next morning by an overexcited Matt who declared he was going to practice playing soccer all day. No prizes for working out why, Skye thought wryly. 'Daddy' featured in practically everything he said.

Luc was already at the playing field when they arrived. Matt, of course, had spotted the red Ferrari in the parking lot, so there was absolutely no sense of disappointment to suffer through. The only suffering was done by Skye, continually torn by Luc's and Matt's pleasure in each other and the fear that she had made a big mistake in not enforcing the limits she had imposed on their relationship.

Yet could the damage be limited, if damage there was going to be? Did time limits mean anything when emotions were involved—emotions that were probably heightened because there wasn't constant contact. Wasn't it said, absence made the heart grow fonder?

Watching Matt adoring his father for the caring interest and the soccer advice Luc was giving him as they watched other boys play their games, Skye could barely contain surges of heightened emotion herself. It was all too easy to fall in love with Luc Peretti. Hard experience could bolster her will to fight her feelings, but Matt didn't know how, wouldn't understand why there was any necessity to shield himself from possible hurt. She found herself violently thinking she would kill Luc if he ever let Matt down.

There were a hundred and sixty five-year-olds to be graded into teams. Short games were organised for the coaches to view and judge levels of talent. When Matt's rostered game came up, he ran onto the field with eager anticipation, determined to show how good he was at running after and kicking the soccer ball.

Luc grinned at her as they were left standing on the sidelines. 'Keen, isn't he?'

'Very,' she dryly agreed. And to stop Luc from assuming too much from the relaxation of rules today, she added, 'Once they start playing in earnest the soccer matches will be on Saturday.'

His day.

The grin faded into an ironic little smile. 'My Sundays are not full of other things, Skye. I'd much prefer to spend them with you.'

'That would be cutting yourself off from the life you've led these past six years,' she said, trying desperately for a matter-of-fact tone.

'I'm far more interested in a life with you and Matt,' he returned without the slightest hesitation for second thoughts.

Her eyes begged him to be honest. 'We don't belong in your world, Luc.'

'Are you saying I must give up everything else to have you and Matt?'

Her heart skipped at the intense purpose he loaded into his question. Would he do it? But surely he would regret it if he did, regret it and blame her for forcing such a decision in years to come.

She sucked in a quick breath and answered, 'No.

I'm just saying we're prisoners of our different backgrounds and it's foolish not to recognise that reality.'

His mouth quirked into a mocking smile. 'You'd be surprised how little my background means to me. You hit the nail on the head in calling it a prison—an oppressive prison I wish to be free of.'

She shook her head. 'It's not how you're acting, Luc. The bonds are very tight. You're pressuring your parents to accept us and they won't.'

'I'm simply giving them the chance, Skye.'

'You're using force.'

'No. Just telling them I've made my choice. Whether they want to live with it or not is up to them.'

'You're prepared to walk away from everything you've known?' She couldn't believe it.

He looked back at her with a searing blaze of unwavering resolution. 'If I have to, yes.'

Her heart turned over. All her resistance to him melted under the heat of wildly hopeful desires, suddenly let loose from the restrictions she had placed on them. He reached out and took her hand, interlacing her fingers with his, gripping hard, and it felt as though he was providing an anchor that would hold her from breaking adrift in any storm.

'Don't doubt my commitment to you and Matt, Skye,' he said, his voice a low throb that drummed on and on in her head. 'Don't doubt it for a second.'

The referee's whistle blew, alerting them to the start of Matt's game. The soccer ball was kicked from the centre line and then there was a blur of boys racing after it. Skye was far too conscious of Luc's grip on her to concentrate on picking Matt out of the melee.

She could not stop herself from wanting this link with him. It felt good—warm, firm, secure. Maybe it was because she'd been alone for too long and Luc was Matt's father. He was also the only man she had ever loved and he was here for her, here for the child they'd made together, too. They should be together.

'Go for it, Matt!'

Luc's yell snapped Skye out of her thoughts. She saw Matt streaking ahead of the other boys, chasing down the ball which had been kicked towards the goal-posts. He reached it first, dribbled it away from the reach of the goalie who had run out to pick it up, then shot it into the net.

'Goal!' Luc yelled, releasing Skye's hand to throw his arms up in accolade to Matt's triumph—a triumph that beamed from his little boy face as he turned to see if they'd been watching and he instantly copied Luc's action, the shared joy of it making the triumph even better.

Skye clapped so hard her hands hurt. 'Well done, Matt!' she called and he trotted back proudly to the centre of the field to start play again.

'That's our son!' Luc said just as proudly, throwing one of his lowered arms around Skye's shoulders and hugging her close. 'Fastest boy on the field and proving he's a striker.'

What if he'd been the slowest and a dud at soccer, Skye thought. But he wasn't so there was no point in thinking it. She doubted Matt was going to be a dud at anything. He was Luc's son.

And hers.

Parents together.

Luc rubbed his cheek over her hair and murmured, 'Marry me, Skye. This is how it should be.'

She wanted to say yes. Being held so close to him, her whole body yearned for the intimacy that could bind them much closer. But the fears she had of consequences could not be banished.

'Give it time, Luc,' she muttered, ducking her head to break the yearning she felt coming from the caress of his cheek.

'Well, at least that's not a no,' he said on a sigh of satisfaction, and dropped his arm from her shoulder to take her hand again, squeezing it possessively. 'I'm here to stay, Skye. The sooner you realise that, the sooner we can become a family.'

That might be true.

But Skye couldn't bring herself to risk making any commitment to him when they'd only spent a couple of days together.

There was a long future ahead of them.

Let Luc prove what he said.

CHAPTER NINE

LUC rolled up the designs for the new apartment complex he'd been working on and set about clearing his desk. Today was the last day of Matt's first school term. Tomorrow was Good Friday. Soccer on Saturday. And on Monday…an elated grin broke out on his face at the thought of it…on Monday he was flying Skye and Matt up to the Gold Coast in Queensland for a family vacation.

Skye's lack of trust in him had been his trump card in breaking down her resistance to the plan. As a *separated* parent, he was entitled to have his son for a week of any school vacation. A family law court would certainly grant it to him. It was an argument that couldn't be refuted but she was afraid of how he might use the time with Matt.

The power of the Peretti family weighed on her mind and he couldn't blame her for worrying about what might happen if he introduced Matt to them behind her back. Not that he would, and the fear wasn't spoken, but her tension over letting Matt out of her sight for so long and the very negative emphasis she'd previously laid on his family background, left Luc in no doubt about how she thought and felt.

It also assured him she would be tempted by his invitation to supervise every moment Matt was with him. He'd produced an internet printout on the *three-*bedroom penthouse apartment he'd booked, plus printouts on the major tourist attractions they could take Matt to—Sea World, Warner Bros. Movie World, Dream World…a family fun vacation all laid out to both of them so Matt's eagerness for his mother to accompany them, and the lure of sharing in her son's new adventures, added to the winning package.

'*Three* bedrooms,' she'd said pointedly, denying the other temptation he had very much on his mind.

'Definitely three,' he assured her, though he privately wanted only two to be used.

He intended a very deliberate seduction this time—no driven quickness about any of the lovemaking. Once he had Skye contentedly sharing his bed, feeling thoroughly loved, the step to marriage should not be such a difficult one for her to take. He wanted her as his wife. And Matt was not the only child he wanted to have.

He fiercely resented having missed out on his son's birth, his babyhood, the toddler years. After he and Skye were married… Luc checked his own eagerness as he realised he knew nothing about how Matt's birth had been for her, whether she would be keen to have more children.

They'd had such little private time to talk—mostly small snatches he'd deliberately manoeuvred. Skye avoided being alone with him whenever she could. Avoidance, however, would be much more difficult for her while staying in the same apartment for a week. After Matt went to bed…

Luc's train of thought was abruptly broken by his father's unheralded arrival—no call from his secretary, the office door swept open, and in he stepped with all the arrogant hauteur of a man who took authority as though it was his right.

Luc felt himself bristling into attack mode and deliberately adopted a relaxed air, leaning back in the chair behind his desk and viewing his father with whimsical curiosity. 'To what do I owe the honour of this visit?' he drawled.

Since their confrontation over Skye at the Bellevue Hill mansion two months ago, they had only met in boardroom meetings with nothing but business on the agenda. Only current and future property development projects were discussed between them, across a table with all other heads of departments present.

His father viewed him now with barely contained impatience, obviously frustrated by Luc's stubborn and rebellious stand against conforming to expectations. 'We will be celebrating Easter Sunday as usual this year,' he stated tersely.

Which meant a big gathering of Italian families for a highly festive lunch. 'I'm glad Mamma feels up to it,' Luc answered dryly.

His father's mouth tightened in anger. 'I'm amazed you have any consideration for her feelings since you haven't seen fit to give her the comfort of a visit or a call.'

'I've been too long on a one-way street with consideration of feelings, Dad. When it starts to go two ways...'

'She is still grieving over Roberto.'

'Then I'm not the son she wants with her, am I?'

'You are the only son she has now.'

'Don't expect me to dance to that tune. Especially not on Roberto's grave.'

'He was your brother.' The emphatic reminder was meant to sting and it did.

'More your son than my brother,' Luc flared back, losing his cool. 'His allegiance was to you, not to me. He sold me out for your approval.'

'He saved you from folly,' his father thundered.

Luc sucked in a quick breath and forced himself to contain the violent emotions surging through him. There was no point in arguing against entrenched prejudice. Waste of time and breath. 'Have you said all you want to say?' he asked in a calmer tone.

He watched his father fight an inner war before coming to the conclusion that it was time to shift ground before bad blood was irrevocably spilled. 'Your mother expects you to lunch on Sunday,' he tossed out as though he himself disdained any need for his surviving son's presence at the family table.

'Are Skye and Matt invited?'

'They are not,' he snapped, refusing to give a moment's consideration to the challenge.

Which was just as well, Luc thought, because he doubted he could persuade Skye into any meeting with his parents at this early juncture. 'Then I won't be there,' he stated unequivocally.

It earned a furious glare. 'Your mother will be disappointed.'

'I'm sorry for her disappointment but it is of your making, Dad. Let's get this in precise perspective.'

'Perspective!' His father snorted in disgust. 'I can only hope your blindness soon passes.'

With the satisfaction of having the last word, he walked out, slamming the door shut behind him.

Luc was somewhat surprised to find he didn't care

how his parents viewed his absence. All his life he had attended their parties, been a focus of their pride and pleasure. He'd actually fed their expectations of him. And been liberally rewarded for it.

But taking Skye from him...taking Matt from him...it had killed any consideration he might have had for their feelings. He didn't want to be with them. He wasn't sure he ever wanted to be with them again...certainly not without Skye and Matt at his side, and both of them being welcomed into their company.

Easter Sunday...

No doubt he would be missed and his absence commented upon by family friends, much to the chagrin of his parents, but for Luc, Easter Sunday was simply the day he had to live through before he could take Skye and Matt away with him for a whole week together. He would quite happily stay in his Bondi Beach apartment; planning, anticipating, gearing himself up to win what he wanted to win.

He stared at the door his father had shut and felt the world he had belonged to receding from him, losing its influence, losing its importance. He suspected the longer he stayed away from it, the less it would mean to him. In fact, it hadn't meant much for a long time—just old familiar connections that had floated through the emptiness of his life after his family had got rid of Skye. He'd given them his courtesy and attention but would he really miss them?

He didn't need them.

He needed Skye.

And their son.

Though he couldn't deny there was also a bitterly burning need in him to have the injustice done to them acknowledged by his parents—acknowledged and redressed!

CHAPTER TEN

ANOTHER day of guilty pleasures, Skye thought as she stood under the shower in her ensuite bathroom, using the expensive perfumed soap which came supplied with all the other luxury items in the penthouse apartment. Luc was paying for everything—absolutely everything—and she shouldn't really be riding along on his vacation with Matt, taking all he was giving.

First class seats on the flight—Matt's first ride in an aeroplane.

More than first class accommodation—every possible comfort, plus wonderful ocean views and the big screen television set in the living room was connected to pay TV, luxury indeed for Matt who was fascinated by the huge variety of shows he could watch.

Yesterday they'd had a marvellous time at Sea World—seeing the awesome Polar bears, watching the fun-loving seals and actually having shallow water encounters with dolphins. And Matt had had enormous fun today, playing with the Looney Tunes characters in the Splash Zone at Warner Bros. Movie World.

She, too, was enjoying herself—couldn't deny it—yet she had the uncomfortable sense of being put in Luc's debt, despite his insistence that he owed her far more than he could ever repay. Worse than that was the secret pleasure of simply being with him. It wasn't just sharing the joy of watching their son have the time of his life. The more time she spent with Luc, the more he reminded her of everything she had loved about him.

It was extremely difficult to keep her focus on Matt. Not difficult…impossible! she ruefully corrected herself. Even here, in the shower, just running the soap over her naked body was stirring sensual memories of how Luc had once caressed her, making her feel how much she missed having that kind of intimacy with him.

He certainly wanted it. There was no mistaking the simmering desire in his eyes whenever he looked at her, whether they were sharing some mutual pleasure in Matt or having a practical discussion on what they were to eat for their next meal. No direct reference was made to it, not by her, not by him. However, the simmering did keep her on edge, trying to ensure nothing she said or did turned up the heat.

The mental cage she'd put around her own feelings for Luc was being continually rattled. The physical attraction was reinforced every time he touched her—a protective arm around her waist in a crowd, a courteous taking of her arm when entering a restaurant, holding her hand—and Matt's—as they walked along together. There was nothing overtly sexual about any of it, yet it subtly made her acutely aware of wanting more from him.

Marry me…

Skye wished it could be as simple as that. She couldn't bring herself to believe it, not with her past experience of the Peretti family. Luc might think he was in control of all the complex factors that would come into play if a marriage between them did take

place, but she could feel their shadows in the background, waiting to grow more and more substance,
threatening to strangle whatever happiness they might
have together.

Besides which, she couldn't help having doubts
about Luc's motivation for a marriage with her. It
wasn't a clear-cut case of loving her, loving Matt,
wanting them to be together. She felt the payback
element very strongly—people being manipulated, including herself, which made her very uneasy about
accepting anything at face value.

Sexual chemistry was something else.

Luc was certainly right about its not going away.

With a wistful sigh, Skye finished washing herself,
turned off the shower, and reached for the lovely soft
bath towel—another luxury to revel in—another guilt,
wrapping herself in what Luc's wealth provided. This
kind of living where cost was no object to every material pleasure was horribly seductive. And could very
easily become addictive.

Did Luc mean it to be?

Was it another form of manipulation to get his own
way?

A one-week family vacation, showing her a bed of
roses…

No vacation was real life, Skye firmly told herself,
more like a dream…time out of time. She had to keep
remembering that, not let it influence her into glossing
over the thorns in the situation with Luc's family.

Although it was mid-April, the days were still hot
and the evenings balmy on the Gold Coast. Skye
chose to slip into her white and brown sundress, wanting to feel cool and relaxed after wearing rather sticky

jeans all day. It was also a relief to brush out her hair from the pinned top-knot and she left it loose. Luc had gone out to get takeaway for dinner tonight so she didn't bother with sandals, padding out to the living-room barefoot to check on Matt.

Having already supervised his bath and put him in pyjamas, she'd left him esconced in front of the television, happily watching a channel which only showed cartoons. He was still there, although now there was a pizza box beside him, and he was eating a big slice dripping with melted cheese and a tomato base.

'Not waiting for us?' she asked in surprise. Luc had made a big thing of having meals together.

'I'm hungry and Daddy said I could have it here,' Matt informed her between bites. 'He's just gone to have a shower. There's a whole lot of stuff in the kitchen,' he added in case she was hungry, too, and couldn't wait.

'I'll check it out.'

Matt's attention was already glued to the screen again, happily engrossed in watching more antics from the Looney Tunes characters.

Skye moved into the kitchen, expecting to find other pizza boxes. All the ingredients for a very tasty salad were sitting on the sink—lettuce, tomato, capsicum, avocado, cucumber, a bottle of Italian dressing. A loaf of twisted bread, made with cheese and spinach, sat on an oven tray ready to be heated up. Slabs of rump steak were being marinaded on a meat plate, and a covered plastic dish containing ten little chat potatoes with butter and parsley was waiting to be put into the microwave oven. Pizza was clearly not on their menu tonight.

'Thought we'd have a proper meal instead,' Luc said, breezing into the kitchen, barefoot like herself, and wearing a fresh pair of white shorts with a brightly coloured Hawaiian shirt he hadn't bothered to button up.

The air was sucked straight out of Skye's lungs. The mental cage flew open and the wild beast of desire flexed its muscles and ran riot through her entire body. Muscles quivered or contracted. Her pulse-rate hopped, skipped and jumped. Heat zoomed through her bloodstream. Her skin tingled. Even her scalp tingled. And her breasts tightened and strained against the cups of cotton that kept them contained.

The blast of virile masculinity was so strong it took an act of will to stop staring, turn her back on it and find enough presence of mind to say, 'I'll wash the lettuce.'

'I'll go set the table out on the balcony,' Luc said cheerfully, busying himself collecting plates and cutlery. 'Best to eat there where we can chat over dinner without the noise and distraction of Matt's cartoons.'

Chat… Skye clung to that word as her hands automatically went to work, tearing off lettuce leaves, running the water in the sink.

Luc had stopped her from retreating into her bedroom the first evening they were here, pleading that he knew nothing of the years he'd missed with Matt and asking her to fill him in on them—such a reasonable request it was only fair to oblige him.

Last night he had drawn her out about her own life since they'd been parted—her mother's death, the move from Caringbah to Brighton-Le-Sands, building up a clientele for her massage business. Only when he'd asked about future plans had she felt it was time to excuse herself and retire, conscious that he now dominated any thinking about the future, making it too slippery a subject. She didn't want to fall into the dangerous trap of discussing marriage with him.

What did Luc have planned for tonight?

Should she plead a headache and escape?

The brief breathing space while he was out on the balcony was not long enough to get the panic at her own vulnerability to him under control. On returning, he headed straight to the refrigerator, just as she was lifting a salad bowl out of the kitchen cupboard next to it, and it felt like a whirlwind coming at her, intent on catching her up in it.

But he didn't touch her. He grinned as he opened the refrigerator door, tossing nothing but companionable words at her. 'Managed to buy a fine bottle of Chardonnay as well, already chilled. Might as well pour us a drink now. It won't take me long to grill the steaks.'

Wine!

Adding an intoxicant to the chaos in her head was not a good idea, but Skye had accepted a glass of wine on the flight up here, and at the restaurants where they'd dined the past two evenings. Refusing one now might alert Luc to a difference in her mood—one she didn't want to explain. Besides, she could sip sparingly. Better not to make an issue of it.

'Thanks,' she said, forcing a smile.

'I remembered how you liked cheesecake, too,' he went on, his eyes dancing with pleasure in his planning. 'Bought two slices with a mango topping and a jar of cream to have for sweets.'

He was remembering more than cheesecake, Skye thought, and making her remember, too. 'You have been busy,' she said dryly, moving back to the sink with the bowl, ready to attack the other vegetables to put in the salad. 'I thought you were getting us pizzas.'

'Impulsive change of mind,' he excused.

With a lot more impulses involved!

'Hope you approve,' he added, his voice loaded with persuasive appeal.

'It's fine, Luc,' she obliged, recognising there was no reasonable argument against what he'd done. Normal politeness forced her to say, 'And special thanks for the cheesecake. I'll enjoy it.'

He set her glass of wine on the bench beside the sink. Still no attempt at touching. There was absolutely nothing Skye could object to in his behaviour. Nor in his dress which she had to admit was as appropriate as her own for an evening at home on the Gold Coast—cool, casual, relaxed.

And Luc did appear to be completely relaxed as he went about cooking what had to be cooked, meat under the griller, bread in the oven, potatoes in the microwave, chatting to her about the day they'd just spent together, acting like a happy father who'd given his son a special treat, *acting like a happy husband sharing it all with his wife…before they shared a lot more in bed.*

Skye couldn't get that last thought out of her head.

The buzz of anticipation *was* in the air, charged with so much sexual electricity she was amazed to find she had actually prepared the salad and tossed the dressing through it, which gave her the chance to escape from the highly charged intimacy of working in the kitchen with Luc. She carried the bowl out to the balcony and paused there long enough to take several deep breaths of fresh sea air.

Nothing was going to happen unless she let it happen.

Skye fixed this maxim firmly in her mind in a desperate effort to counteract the rampant desires that were clamouring to sneak right past it, whispering their tempting promises of pleasure, insidiously urging her to satisfy more than a weakness for cheesecake, demanding to know why shouldn't she take what was on offer? It didn't commit her to marriage.

'Lovely evening, isn't it?'

Her heart jolted at the realisation Luc was just behind her. She whipped around from the balcony railing, gearing up to fight off any move on her, only to find him standing on the other side of the table, setting down an ice bucket containing the bottle of wine.

'Yes, it is,' she choked out, hoping she didn't look alarmed.

Was it all in *her* mind?

He smiled, watching the light sea breeze gently lifting the silky fan of her hair around her shoulders.

No, it wasn't just her.

The smile was very sensual. And satisfaction glinted in his eyes as he said, 'Matt's fallen asleep on the floor. Shall I carry him in to bed?'

Out of the way. No possible distraction from a little boy who was totally worn out from the day's excitement, too exhausted to care where he slept. Had that been planned, too?

'I'll do it while you finish up in the kitchen,' Skye answered, wanting the activity, anything to put space between her and Luc.

'Okay.' He shrugged and retreated.

Skye followed him inside. Matt had simply toppled over beside the pizza box, not even a cushion under his head. He didn't stir when she gathered him up in her arms and remained a dead weight as he was carried into his bedroom, head lolling on her shoulder, arms and legs limp. She laid him down on the pillow, manouevred his body in between the sheets, tucked him in and dropped a kiss on his forehead.

There was not so much as a flutter of consciousness from Matt. He was completely at peace, leaving it up to his parents to take care of his future.

Skye wished she had a crystal ball to look into and see the consequences of all the futures that could radiate out from this point in her life. Right now she was just meeting each day as it came, trying to evade any decisions which might commit her to a course that would put Matt and herself in a bad place. It would be so easy to shift all the responsibility on to Luc, to surrender them both into his keeping, for better or for worse, but she'd come too far on her own to give up all control.

Somehow she had to see her way more clearly. Luc had been asking about Matt's life and hers. Since she had to get through the next hour or two with him, why not ask about his life? Up until now she had shied away from showing any personal interest in him, sensing he would seize some advantage from it, draw her into knowing more than she would feel comfortable with.

Her mouth curved in black irony as she turned away from Matt and caught sight of her reflection in the mirrors covering the doors of the built-in cupboard. It was not the reflection of a woman who felt comfortable with anything.

Her eyes were wide and anxious. Her shoulders were stiff, carrying too many burdens. Her hair looked undisciplined, floating free. And while it might not be discernible to other eyes, the ache in her body—screaming to be soothed—seemed to be telegraphed from every taut curve outlined by the too skimpy dress.

Bad choice!

She should have worn a less *inviting* outfit. Though her reaction to Luc would have been the same. It was too late to change now—too obvious a move, telling Luc how deeply disturbed she was by him. Better to concentrate on using tonight to find out where he was coming from, where he might take her to if she weakened.

She forced her legs to take her out of the shelter of Matt's bedroom. The stark truth was…there was no hiding place from Luc Peretti. If he wasn't present physically, he was certainly in her mind. Everything he represented had to be faced, sooner or later. Postponing the evil hour wouldn't help one bit.

The television was still playing cartoons. She found the remote control panel and turned it off. The abrupt fall of silence prompted her to wryly imagine a drumroll, heralding curtain up. The stage had definitely been set. The waft of warm bread was enough to tease an appetite. No doubt Luc would set the ball rolling on action. What she had to do was catch the ball and direct some action herself.

'Ready, Skye?' he called from the kitchen.

'Yes,' she replied. 'Do you need a hand with anything?'

'No. I'm serving now. Go on out to the table and I'll be with you in a minute.'

She did as he directed since it suited her, as well. The table was round, big enough to seat six, not so wide that sitting opposite each other was an awkward distance but wide enough to prevent any easy physical touching. As long as she sat down, she was safe.

Skye sat.

The bread was being kept warm under a tea-cloth. Their glasses were filled with wine. The salad and potatoes were handy for self-serving. Luc came striding out with their steaks on a plate, placing it on the centre of the table with a flourish, inviting her to help herself.

He sat down, grinning from ear to ear. 'Isn't this nice?' he said.

It was…if the circumstances had been anywhere near normal. 'Yes. Thank you,' Skye replied, feeling swamped by the power of the man.

The dinner was irrelevant.

His eyes said he wanted to eat her up.

And in her heart of hearts, Skye knew she wanted to be eaten by Luc Peretti.

CHAPTER ELEVEN

SILENCE was the enemy. The romantic setting, Luc smiling at her, the sense of sharing an intimate dinner…silence seeded the longing to forget the lost years, forget what had parted them, slide back into that time of innocence when their joy in each other overwhelmed everything else, making the differences between them irrelevant.

Skye forced herself to plunge into conversation, instinctively targeting his family connection, needing to keep in the forefront of her mind why she couldn't allow herself to be tempted into setting it aside.

'What does your work entail these days, Luc?' she asked, forcing herself into normal action as well, piling some salad and a couple of potatoes onto her plate.

'Still designing buildings, though I'm now head of that department,' he answered easily, waiting for her to finish serving herself before doing the same.

'A fast rise,' she commented. He'd been a junior architect in the Peretti Corporation six years ago.

'I could say I had the talent and the brain for it,' he drawled with arrogant confidence.

'Not to mention being Maurizio Peretti's oldest son.'

The good humour instantly left his face, his expression hardening into cold pride, his dark eyes sharply challenging. 'You don't think I've earned my place?'

It pulled Skye back from the black judgement she had made. Because his family had not been fair to her, was no reason why she shouldn't be fair to Luc. 'I think you're capable of doing whatever you set out to do,' she said slowly. 'I just meant…well, you are tied to your father. Weren't both you and Roberto educated and groomed to fit into the places he planned for you to take?'

Architecture, engineering…perfect for a business centred on property development.

'I can't answer for Roberto who may well have pursued what pleased my father,' he said sardonically, 'but I was always interested in design, Skye, and chose my own career.'

Yes, he would, she realised, just as he had chosen to continue a relationship with her, despite his parents' disapproval. Only damning evidence of the worst infidelity she could have committed had stopped him. Luc was not his father's tool, yet being so strongly connected to the family business did leave him vulnerable to manipulation, and blood ties were not easily broken.

He felt he'd earned his place, was proud of filling it, probably with distinction—an important cog in the Peretti wheel. He wouldn't want to walk away from it. Skye suspected he'd fight to keep it, which could mean deadly conflict with his father who would definitely be opposed to the marriage Luc wanted. And she and Matt would be the meat in the sandwich.

Not a happy prospect.

'I report to my father at boardroom meetings but I

don't work under him,' Luc tossed at her to elucidate the situation. 'I have autonomy within my department.'

'Autonomy…' Skye seized on that word as though it was a lifeline out of the frightening problems that had been whirling through her brain.

It meant Luc was his own boss. He couldn't be manipulated where business judgements were concerned. And it was probably faulty reasoning to attach what had happened with the damning photographs to what might develop in his work situation. Emotional judgements were in a far more volatile territory.

'I'm sorry for implying…you could be pushed around,' she rushed out, suddenly feeling very much on the wrong foot. 'I guess your father is…something of a bogey-man to me.'

His face relaxed, his eyes softening to sympathetic understanding. 'I don't live in my father's pocket, Skye. He can't buy me away from you and Matt.'

Embarrassment—or was it something else? A deep treacherous pleasure?—sent a flood of heat to her cheeks. The commitment—conviction—in his voice, the possessive warmth in his eyes, the unswerving sense of purpose engulfing her… Skye teetered on the edge of giving him her trust, wanting him to take care of everything: her, Matt, the future…

She barely brought herself back from the brink, finding a brittle escape in focusing on the food on her plate, telling herself to keep talking.

Silence was the enemy.

Luc was filling it with temptations.

She was not even clear on why she had to fight them any more.

'What are you working on at the moment?' she asked, hoping his answer would be long and distracting.

He obligingly described his current project. The company had bought up old boatyards along the harbour shore at Balmain and Luc was designing a new apartment complex to be built on the site. She listened to the pleasure and satisfaction in his voice as he explained what he wanted constructed and how it would take advantage of the view, as well as catering for every modern aspect of living in the city.

Clearly he enjoyed his work and the opportunity to have such lavish projects to work on. He might not recognise how deeply he was tied to the Peretti Corporation since it had always been there for him to step into, but Skye did.

Big money at his fingertips.

Big money to invest how he saw fit.

Big money to spend how he pleased in his private life, as well.

As long as he stayed where he belonged.

Or was that being unfair, too? Luc had more than enough driving force to succeed in establishing himself anywhere, in any company, or on his own. Why couldn't she just accept that he didn't live in his father's pocket?

Because she couldn't make the fear go away.

It was too deeply rooted in past pain.

'Do you still live at Cronulla?' she asked, needing to know if he'd continued living with his family in the incredibly luxurious horseshoe compound facing the waterfront there.

He shook his head. 'Dad sold that place five years ago.'

The timing made Skye wonder if Maurizio Peretti had decided to shift his family right away from the neighbouring suburb of Caringbah where Luc's illegitimate child was possibly far too close for comfort.

Luc flashed her an ironic look. 'He upgraded to a heritage-listed mansion at Bellevue Hill.'

Mega-bucks, she thought, plus getting way out of the range of any accidental meeting with the unsuitable woman and her child.

'Big enough to house three generations of the family,' Luc went on, his voice carrying a sardonic edge.

Everything within Skye recoiled at the idea of living in the same house with his parents. It would be absolute madness to even consider marrying Luc if it meant co-habiting with his family. Regardless of how attractive he was to her, how good he was to Matt…

'It hasn't worked out that way,' he said, forestalling the tortured impulse to reject his proposal here and now.

'Oh?' It was more a choked gasp than a query. Skye was appalled at how wildly hope had galloped over despair.

'Roberto obligingly brought his bride home—' Luc's riveting dark eyes glittered derisively '—the bride my father had hand-picked for me, except I didn't oblige.'

'So Roberto married her instead?' She shook her head, shocked that such a switch would be made in so serious a life commitment.

Luc shrugged. 'He was happy to. And I'm sure Gaia found Roberto a more charming husband than I would have been. Besides which, it was a very advantageous marriage on both sides. Unfortunately, even the best-laid plans can go astray. Gaia was still childless when Roberto died, and has since returned to her own family.'

'You're not expected to…to console his widow?'

'I doubt my father would wish me to take a wife who might not be able to produce the grandchildren he wants,' he answered cynically. 'Gaia suffered two miscarriages in her short marriage to Roberto.'

It was revolting to Skye to think of any woman being regarded as a baby-making machine. On the other hand, Roberto's wife had probably been sadly disappointed herself not to have had a much-wanted child.

'I'm sure your father can find you another suitable wife for his dynastic ambitions,' she tossed at Luc, knowing she should never take on that role herself.

'I won't marry anyone but you, Skye.'

His eyes burned with unshakeable purpose, making her too agitated to even pretend to eat any more. She put down her knife and fork, willing herself to face him with her own determination. 'It won't work,' she stated bluntly.

He set down his cutlery and focused on her, the whole concentrated power of his energy coming at her full blast. 'I'll make it work.'

She leaned forward, fighting for her independence again. 'If you think, for one moment, I'd live under the same roof as…'

'I don't live there myself,' he added. 'I moved out when Roberto married. Bought my own apartment at Bondi Beach.'

Her mind whirled at this apparent disconnection to his family, though it quickly seized on the fact that the suburb of Bondi was right next to Bellevue Hill. 'Not far from them,' spilled from her mouth.

'Far enough to have separate lives,' he retorted.

Separate... Skye paused to catch her breath. Was she making bogey-men of everything, snatching at whatever fed her fear of the power his family had to hurt? Luc was proving at every point he was his own man. And he had been hurt, too, by the dreadful deception that had been played to make him turn his back on her.

'Why did you move out?' she asked, wondering if there had been some earlier rift between him and his family.

He shrugged. 'I didn't care to have the happiness of Roberto's marriage rubbed in my face every day.'

Her insecurities surged again. 'Regrets for rejecting it yourself, Luc?'

'None at all. I wished my brother well with it.'

'Then why did it upset you?'

'It didn't upset me. I knew my father would constantly use it as leverage to get me to fall into line with his plans, which would end up being unpleasant for everyone, so I removed myself from the situation.'

'While still maintaining your relationship with your family,' she said, pressing to ascertain just how important it was to him.

'I had the choice of coming and going as I pleased.'

'Did you ever miss a special family occasion?'

'I just did.'

Again she felt her defensive mat being swept out

from under her feet. 'What was it?' she asked, needing to know how much it meant.

His eyes glittered a joyless challenge. 'You remember the Easter Sunday luncheon you attended with me six years ago?'

The memory leapt vividly to mind—the huge luncheon party, and feeling like a fish out of water amongst all the Italian families, people engaging Luc in conversation and subtly ignoring her presence. Not obvious snubs, but definitely left out in the cold while warmth was overflowing everywhere else. It had been such a relief when Roberto had taken the time to charm her out of her sense of alienation.

Luc's brother…setting up the trap to get rid of her.

'You haven't told me how Roberto died.'

Luc frowned.

Realising she'd thrown him off-stride, Skye bitterly reminded him of the person who had betrayed them both. 'He was *nice* to me that Easter Sunday, making me feel welcome when no one else did.'

There was a flash of pain in his eyes. 'I'm sorry…sorry I subjected you to…' He shook his head. 'It won't happen again, Skye. I swear it. I won't take you anywhere near my family without an assurance that you will be welcomed.' He looked at her with searing intensity as he gave her his personal assurance. 'And I'd be watching. Watching every minute. If you're made to feel uncomfortable—'

'I would feel uncomfortable anyway, Luc,' she cut in bleakly.

He nodded, not pressing. 'You might find that Matt will break the ice,' he said hopefully.

She couldn't help thinking their only hope of having any happiness together was in living separate lives to his family. And was that really a possibility?

'Roberto died of extensive injuries from a car accident,' Luc said, grimacing as he softly added, 'He did regret what he'd done, Skye.'

'Not while he had his life to live,' she pointed out, her eyes sadly mocking Luc's view of the situation. 'I don't think your father is ever going to accept me.'

'I'd like to give him the time to take that option.'

'Time won't make any difference. I'm sure you challenged him over this Easter Sunday, asking if Matt and I would be welcome. He wouldn't come at it, would he?'

'I don't expect a quick turnaround. But the point was made, Skye.'

'And he made his. You're welcome. I'm not.'

Ruthless steel answered her. 'It will be his loss if he doesn't change his attitude.'

Your loss, too, Skye thought, and spelled out the most testing scenario of all. 'What if he threatens to cut you off?'

'So be it.'

Not the slightest dent in the steel. But Skye felt it was pride talking. In his heart of hearts, Luc didn't believe it would happen. To him, the family link was too strong. Blood would tell in the end. It was the argument he'd used to her for his parents' eventual acceptance of Matt as their grandchild. What he didn't take into consideration was how much *they* felt Matt's blood was tainted by hers.

A wave of sheer misery washed through her. Here she was sitting opposite a man she'd loved—a man she still couldn't help loving—the father of her child,

wanting to marry her—and a decision about their future should be simple and straightforward, not
hemmed around with the dark threat of endless pain.

'Skye...'

She had nothing left to say. The grief his family
had already given her was swimming through her
mind, carrying her towards rocks that would smash
any happiness she might achieve with Luc. It startled
her when his chair scraped back. Her heart leapt er-
ratically as he rose to his feet, his eyes blazing with
savage emotion.

'*You* come first with me!' he hurled at her, using
his voice like a hammer, forcefully intent on breaking
through anything that held him out of the centre of
her existence.

The words rang in Skye's ears, drowning out the
voices of doom that kept tugging her away from
him...*first with me...first with me*. Not his son. Not
his family. *She came first.*

In a few quick strides he was around the table,
pulling her up from her chair, wrapping her in a fierce
embrace, pouring out passionate pleas.

'Don't reject me, Skye...'

She didn't want to. Her whole body was flooding
with the need to be held by him, loved by him, sur-
rendering so utterly to his embrace, her head nestled
onto his shoulder and her eyes closed to shut out the
rest of the world.

'You know it's good between us. We connect on
levels that no one else even touches.'

It felt good just feeling his chest rising and falling
with each breath he took.

'I made myself forget that, told myself I'd only

imagined it to satisfy some need in me.' Harsh mockery in his voice, then powerful conviction. 'But I only had to meet you again to know we should never have been parted.'

Never echoed in Skye's mind, knocking out all the reasons why they should be parted.

'I've been like a hollow man all these years without you.'

The emptiness left after your heart has been torn out, she thought, and hers had only been punched back into chaotic life when Luc had re-appeared and the fear of being hurt like that again…and she might be…but right now, the need to have him was so paramount, it pushed the fear away to be dealt with some other time. Not now. The emptiness cried out to be filled, filled to overflowing.

'I want to make love to you, Skye.'

Yes…

Her whole body sighed in relief as the constraints she had willed on it were lifted.

Luc's imprisoning embrace eased a little, one arm still possessively pinning her to him while the other hand wove through the long fall of her hair, finding enough purchase to gently tug her head back, tilting it up to his.

'Look at me…'

She opened her eyes to see dark torment in his.

'It's not just sex, Skye. I can get that anywhere. You can, too. Don't belittle what we have together. I want you to remember how it was…how it can still be…'

He carried those last throbbing words to her mouth, making her feel them…how it still was…Luc kissing her, the wild surge of response shooting through her, wanting him so much, wanting all he'd ever given her before, everything so beautifully right between them.

They weren't forceful kisses, no taking in them at all, more a searching for the sense of mutual loving, the desire to establish it was so, overriding any urge to dominate. He was sexually aroused. She was, too. But it didn't matter, just a natural part of what was happening, the yearning of their bodies expressing the need for each other.

'Come to bed with me, Skye.'

It wasn't a command. Nor a plea. It was a softly murmured request for them to move to a private place where nothing else could intrude on the intimacy of being together.

'Yes,' she whispered, rebelling against the inhibitions that warned of consequences she would never be able to control.

The inhibitions sprang from Luc's world, but Luc was here with her, and if she truly came first with him, couldn't she let him come first with her?

He eased back and took her hand in his, leading her off the balcony, leading...not picking her up and carrying her off, letting her feet speak their consent to this move and they did, willingly walking through the apartment to his bedroom, though they faltered when she saw the bed, one high-risk consequence insisting on being acknowledged.

'I'm not protected, Luc.'

'I'll take care of it.'

The smooth reply was meant to soothe away the fear, but it was a sharp reminder that he hadn't cared last time, had actually hoped she'd fallen pregnant.

She turned to face him, her eyes searching for truth. 'Will you?' she asked, needing to know there was no manipulation of her vulnerability intended—no thought of future entrapment. The gift of love should be a free gift, if this was what it was.

He lifted a hand and gently stroked the anxiety from her facial muscles, his eyes promising safety with him as he answered, 'If we make another child, it will only be when we both want to. A planned baby, Skye, not conceived by accident nor a lack of forethought.'

'You came prepared for…for…'

'I hoped.'

'You aimed for it,' she wryly corrected him, running her fingers down the bared strip of chest his unbuttoned shirt had left open for her touch—a temptation beyond bearing any longer.

'Why wouldn't I? You're the woman I want above all others.'

The man she wanted above all others.

He dropped his hand to her shoulder, fingertips drawing the strap of her sundress over to her arm. 'Do you want to stop me, Skye?'

'No.' She sucked in a deep breath, relaxing as it shuddered out again. 'No one can take this away.'

Maybe they could create a small world together—a place of survival for the love they could share, sheltered from the storms that might rage around them, trying to break in and tear them apart.

She wanted it to be possible.

The magic of touching like this…making love…

Was it strong enough to hold against any destructive intrusion?

Or was such a small world an impossible dream,
bred from desires that craved satisfaction?

Skye didn't know.

Didn't want to think.

The need…simply to feel…made everything else
fade away.

CHAPTER TWELVE

Luc found himself in two minds as he drove up to the Bellevue Hill mansion. It had been nine months since he had last set foot in it and he wasn't sure he wanted to make any rapprochement with his parents on a personal level. He might have a happier future with Skye if he kept them shut out of his private life.

Yet family was family.

Business forced him to deal with his father in boardroom meetings where all current property developments were reported on and future projects discussed. The subject of Skye was never mentioned between them. No doubt his father thought if he ignored the bone of contention long enough, it might go away, especially if the woman he regarded as unsuitable did not agree to marry his son. Or given enough time, Luc might have second thoughts about going through with his declared intention.

His mother had not made the effort to contact him—probably still wallowing in grief over Roberto. He had not been inclined to make the effort to visit her, either, remembering all too well her rigid disapproval of Skye—setting a foundation of rejection which Roberto had played on, creating a lethal structure of lies with supposedly just cause.

Luc could not bring himself to sympathise with his mother's grief when he was constantly conscious of the damage his brother had wrought, not to mention the years he'd missed of his own son's life. Besides which, her approval meant nothing to him any more.

He wondered if his mother knew about Matt or had his father *protected* her from any unsettling knowledge of an unwanted grandchild. If he had kept Matt's existence from her, the cat would certainly be out of the bag tonight!

He left his car parked near the front door which was promptly opened by the butler who informed him his parents were in the formal drawing room. Interesting, Luc thought grimly. Having called ahead, he was expected. No doubt his courtesy call had alerted his father to the possibility of serious news behind it so he was getting the grand treatment, designed to impress on him what he might be giving up in going against his parents' wishes.

Futile game-playing. He'd moved beyond any influence his father could bring to bear on him. Even professionally. He could walk away from the Peretti Corporation and start his own business, if necessary.

He didn't wait for the butler to usher him into the drawing room, moving ahead with quick purposeful strides, opening the door himself. His father was standing in front of the marble fireplace, the dominant figure amongst all his prized material possessions. His mother was sitting very upright in a nearby armchair. Still wearing black, he noted, but her regal demeanour telegraphed that her attention could be courted again.

She wore a full complement of jewellery and she'd obviously been to a beauty salon today, her thick wavy grey hair groomed to perfection, not a strand out of place, her fingernails buffed and polished. Her face was skilfully made up to presentation standard and Luc reflected on how imposing she could be when it suited her—totally intimidating to Skye.

'Mamma…more yourself again, I see,' he said dryly, walking forward to confront them more closely.

'No thanks to you, Luciano, since you haven't seen fit to come home for nine months,' his father remonstrated.

He shrugged. 'This isn't my home. You both know where I live…if I was needed,' he added in a pointed drawl.

'It's not a case of need,' came the brusque retort. 'Out of respect for your mother, you should have—'

'He is here now, Maurizio,' his mother broke in, giving Luc a gracious nod. 'Please sit down. It has been a long time.'

He propped himself on the well-cushioned armrest of a sofa, not about to let his father stand over him. 'I assume Dad told you what I've been doing. If you were interested in re-acquainting yourself with Skye Sumner and meeting our son, you could have called me, Mamma.'

Her lips compressed, whether in disapproval or frustration Luc wasn't sure, but clearly his words came as no shock to her. She knew all right. Her gaze turned straight to her husband in a sharp demand for him to deal with it.

Luc waited for his reply, wanting to be clued in on how they viewed the situation. His father wore his poker-face, not giving anything away. His reply was laced with careful diplomacy.

'We felt any *re-acquainting* was best left to you…to make a time…if it was what you wanted.'

So the policy had been to wait. No red carpet welcome was about to be rolled out. Not while ever there was an outside chance that Luc might come to his senses when there was no family support forthcoming, no turnaround to oblige his feelings. A complete stand-off.

Luc eyed his father with open scepticism. 'I did ask at Easter, Dad. You made it clear a meeting was not to your liking.'

'In front of all our friends?' he scoffed as though the idea was absurd.

'You could have put Skye and Matt at ease with you before your guests arrived.'

He waved an angry dismissal. 'The timing was wrong.'

'When will it be right?' Luc mocked. 'The truth is you had Skye unjustly trashed and can't bring yourself to offer her the apology she deserves, let alone acknowledge the beautiful person she is, and has always been.'

It earned a furiously resentful glare.

Luc shook his head and delivered the bottom line. 'If you're waiting for Skye to go away, you'll be waiting the rest of our lives.'

Thin-lipped silence.

His mother's hands fretted at each other as she waited for her husband's next move.

Luc didn't wait. He bluntly called the next move for him. 'You *took,* Dad. As far as I'm concerned, it's up to you—both of you—to come to reasonable terms with what I'm about to take back.'

His mother shifted uneasily, her face showing anxiety as she quickly asked, 'What does that mean?'

'It means that Skye and I are getting married.'

'No! This cannot be!' She rose in agitation, turning in protest to her husband. 'You said this would not happen, Maurizio. You said—'

He sliced a dismissive wave to silence the out-pouring. 'It's not done yet, Flavia.' He turned a frown of intense disapproval to Luc. 'If you must marry this woman…'

'Her name is Skye. Skye Sumner,' Luc repeated, ramming her name down his father's throat.

'…a wedding must be planned…a proper church wedding…'

'More delaying tactics, Dad?'

'You are my son! Your marriage has to be cele-brated in an appropriate manner.'

'Then you should have come to the party earlier. It's taken me all these months to win Skye's trust and I won't throw it away to accommodate a family who has made no gesture towards welcoming her into it. I've finally persuaded her to sign the necessary forms and we'll be getting married as soon as it's legally possible.'

'Which is when?' his father shot at him.

Luc gave a derisive laugh as he straightened up from the armrest. 'So you can use the time to stop it, Dad?' His eyes glittered out and out war. 'Take one step in that direction…'

'Enough!' his mother cried, swinging a fierce gaze from one to the other. 'Enough, Maurizio! I will not lose this son and I want my grandchild. If we have to accept this woman as Luciano's wife, we will.' She turned to Luc with an indomitable air. 'It *must* be a proper wedding with all the families invited. I will see to it myself.'

'Flavia…' Anger at her insubordination.

She rebelled against it, bristling with her own anger as she stated, 'I will not have Luciano shame us by marrying in a clandestine fashion. It is bad enough that his bride is not of the Italian community.'

'With a bastard child,' his father savagely reminded her.

'And whose fault is it that my son was born out of wedlock?' Luc sliced at him.

His father's chin jerked up in aggressive pride, ignoring the accusation to address his wife. 'It cannot be supported, Flavia. I will not support it.'

'You chose a wife for Roberto who could not carry a baby full-term,' she fired back at him. 'Where is our future, Maurizio?'

'In limbo until our son sees sense,' he said in disgust.

'Then in limbo it will stay,' Luc declared with steely resolve.

'Luciano…' his mother pleaded.

'No, Mamma, I will not change my mind. I am sorry to bring you shame by not having a traditional wedding, but you and Dad have chosen to keep Skye alienated, and as long as she remains *this woman* or *that woman* to you, I won't let you near her to plan a wedding or anything else.'

'She has to do it for you or you will be an outcast, Luciano,' came the fierce rejoinder. 'If she loves you…'

'Skye always loved me. And was put through hell for it. Because of any lack of caring from this family, she brought up our son alone. I need to prove my love for her, not the other way around, Mamma.'

'There *was* caring,' she argued. 'Your father set up a trust fund.'

'Which was not administered as it should have been.' He swung a hard gaze to his father. 'Right, Dad?'

'The intention was there,' he tersely countered.

'The intention to keep Skye and my son at a distance. Which you're still doing, regardless of how I feel about it.'

His father threw up his hands in exasperation. 'You were in shock at learning what was done for your own good. Making rash judgements. But to persist in this folly…to turn your back on your family…'

'A family that deceived me? Robbed me of five years of my son's life?'

'Stop!' his mother cried vehemently. 'You are like two bulls locking horns and I will not have it. There is the child to consider, Maurizio. He is our only grandchild.'

'There is Skye to consider, as well, Mamma. I will not let Matt near anyone who doesn't treat his mother with the respect she deserves. He's a happy little boy, very much due to his mother's caring, and I don't want any shadow put on his life. He knows nothing but love…'

'You think I won't love him?' his mother cried in obvious angst at the prospect of being kept from the only grandchild she had.

'I doubt that ignoring and disapproving of his mother will seem like love to Matt. He's a very bright, intelligent child.' Luc couldn't resist proudly adding, 'He could read books, even before he went to school.'

'You hear that, Maurizio? This child you thought would be no good? At five years of age he can read!'

'And he shot more goals at soccer this year than any other boy on his team,' Luc went on, deliberately rubbing in what his father was missing—the game of soccer being one of his passions, as it was with most Italians.

'It is as well you find some joy in the boy because you will find none in this marriage,' his father thundered, refusing to be moved from his stance.

'You're wrong, Dad,' Luc said quietly. 'I feel alive with Skye. She fills the emptiness I've known for far too long.'

'There will be an even greater emptiness when you find yourself ostracised from all the Italian families.'

It would happen, too. His father would make it happen. A line would be drawn, with no crossing over from either side. He remembered the conversation with Skye when she'd said they were prisoners of their backgrounds and he'd expressed a wish to be free of the oppressive constriction of his. She hadn't believed him—it wasn't how he was acting—and he realised now why she'd hung back from committing herself to marrying him.

Because he'd been still hanging on, working for the Peretti Corporation, maintaining at least that professional link, hoping for a change of attitude, a change of heart from his parents, wanting an acceptance of his reality, thinking he could force an acceptance—blindly tied to bonds that had to be broken, proving to Skye he was truly free of them.

An act of love for an act of faith.

He looked at his father who'd ruled so much of his

life, but would rule no more. 'My resignation will be on your desk Monday morning, Dad. Effective immediately.'

'You can't do that!' he blustered, clearly appalled by this decision and seizing on a cogent argument against it. 'You're under contract for the resort in Far North Queensland.'

'Then I'm giving notice that this will be the last contract I'll work on. As soon as it's done…'

'You'll give up everything for this woman?' he yelled, his face reddening with the intensity of his outrage.

Yes, he would.

He'd told Skye he would.

It was well past time he did it.

He shook his head over his father's total lack of understanding of what Skye gave him. There was no point in trying to explain what wouldn't be heard anyway. He simply said, 'I just won't be held by your expectations of me any longer. Your father emigrated to Australia on his own to build a new life for himself, Dad. I can make a new life elsewhere, too.'

'No! No! You must stop this!' his mother broke in again. 'You men and your headstrong pride! You are breaking my heart! Both of you!' She dropped back into her armchair, slumping over, her hands pressed to her chest.

'See what you've done? Upsetting your mother?' His father bellowed at him, striding over to the chair to put a comforting arm around her.

Emotional blackmail.

The weeping and wailing would start any second.

'I'm sorry, Mamma, but this situation was not of

my making,' Luc said, softening his tone while still holding to his own determination. 'We all have choices.' He cast one last look at his father to state unequivocally, 'I've made mine.'

Then he walked out.

Out of the drawing room.

Out of the multi-million dollar mansion.

Out of the lives of his parents.

He could start a new life elsewhere.

And he would.

His own family, making their own friends, completely free of the past.

CHAPTER THIRTEEN

IT WAS there again!

Skye's heart skipped a beat at the sight of the black limousine, parked directly across the street from her house, as it had been each afternoon for the past three days.

Her last client of the day noticed it, too—so totally out of place in this neighbourhood. As out of place as Luc's red Ferrari! 'Is there a wedding?' she asked, trying to find an explanation for its presence.

'I don't know,' Skye answered.

Her client shrugged, stepped off the front porch and headed towards the gate. The limousine had nothing to do with her. Skye couldn't feel quite so dismissive of it. The tinted windows made it impossible to see if anyone was seated inside the car, but she *felt* as though she was being watched.

She quickly shut the door, wishing her anxious tension could be blocked out as easily as the limousine which she found increasingly disturbing. Luc was away this week, having flown up to Cairns in far north Queensland for on-site meetings about a new project. His father would know that. Was someone from the Peretti family behind those tinted windows, looking for ammunition that could be used against her?

There was none.

But that didn't mean it couldn't be manufactured.

Or was she being hopelessly paranoid?

Skye tried to shake off her worry as she threw off her masseur clothes on which she'd spilled some oil, took a shower, then dressed in jeans and T-shirt to go and pick up Matt from school. Only three more weeks now and the school year would be over. Her life here at Brighton-Le-Sands would be over.

Luc wanted to get married before Christmas and once they were, she and Matt would move to his Bondi apartment where they'd live until this last contract with the Peretti Corporation was completed. Then they'd relocate, close to wherever Luc decided to set up business for himself.

It was all settled.

Except the black limousine made her feel unsettled.

Skye decided she would tell Luc about it tonight when he called, as he called every night to chat with her and Matt over the phone. He had informed his family about their forthcoming marriage. Predictably the news had not been met with joy. Luc had insisted it didn't matter. The future he wanted revolved around her and Matt.

Skye believed him. All this year he'd shown he was happy with them, persuading her that a marriage between them was workable, despite his family lurking in the background. His decision to resign from his position in his father's business empire was the ultimate proof of freedom from an influence she'd still feared. It gave her far more confidence in their future together.

But would his family leave them alone?

The limousine was still there when she left the house to walk to Matt's school. She could have driven the Alfa so as not to feel *exposed* to watching eyes, but it was a fine sunny afternoon and it wasn't her habit to drive when a walk would be pleasant. Besides, she had nothing to hide.

Matt was bubbling with news about the end of year school concert. They'd just had a rehearsal for it. His class was doing a selection of nursery rhymes in song and action and he was demonstrating how he twinkled like a star, singing away at the top of his voice as they turned into their street.

The limousine had not moved.

Matt broke off his song to comment, 'The big black car is there again, Mummy.'

'So it is,' she replied, trying to sound careless.

'Maybe a giant lives in it,' he speculated. 'His legs are too long to fit in an ordinary car.'

'You could be right,' Skye lightly agreed while her mind painted in a scary giant, like Maurizio Peretti whose great wealth gave him a very long reach.

'Look, Mummy! The door is opening!' Matt cried excitedly, delighted at the prospect of seeing the occupant.

The driver's door! So someone *was* inside behind the tinted windows! Skye felt herself tensing up but the chauffeur who emerged was not enough in himself to confirm her fears.

'It's just a man in a uniform,' Matt said in disappointment.

The man in the uniform rounded the bonnet of the limousine and opened the far side passenger door, perking up Matt's anticipation again.

'There must be someone else, too.'

Just keep walking, Skye told herself, determined not to be intimidated by the *someone else*.

'It's a lady,' came Matt's surprised commentary.

A lady, indeed, Skye thought bitterly, her spine instantly stiffening as she recognised Luc's mother. No doubt now that the limousine was associated with his family. The chauffeur escorted Flavia Peretti across the street and was dismissed by her when she was safely on the sidewalk, right next to the front gate where Luc had stood waiting, nine months ago.

'Is she coming to our place, Mummy?' Matt asked, curiosity enlivened by this strange visitor who was watching their approach.

'Maybe she wants to ask for directions, Matt,' Skye temporised, unsure what to expect from this meeting and unwilling to expose her son to a relationship that might prove harmful.

Flavia Peretti looked very imposing, elegantly dressed in black, her hair more grey than Skye remembered, though perfectly groomed as always. She had a strong-boned face and a very upright figure, tall enough to carry her weight well, very much an Italian Mamma, although the softness of her womanly curves belied the hardness of her judgemental character. She was staring at Matt, just as Luc had done—the son of her son, her only grandchild.

'Why is she looking at me?' Matt asked.

'Perhaps you remind her of someone,' Skye answered, worrying that an introduction was about to be forced.

And then what?

Her stomach was churning. Her mind was, too. Why had Flavia Peretti come now? What was the point of this visit? To try to stop her from marrying Luc? To get to her while her precious son was away, destroy her trust in their love?

All Skye's protective instincts told her to keep Matt out of any confrontation with Luc's mother. Needing to distract attention away from her son, as soon as they were close enough, she called out, 'Can I help you?'

Flavia Peretti lifted her gaze from Matt, looking at Skye with a determined directness that mocked any pretence of not knowing who she was. 'Miss Sumner...' she started, letting her own identification of Skye hang for a moment.

'Yes? Do you want to make an appointment?' Skye rushed out, hoping the evasive tactic might raise a decent sense of discretion. She put her hand pointedly on Matt's shoulder as they paused by the gate, waiting for an answer.

The intense dark eyes, so very like Luc's, flashed a rueful understanding. 'If I may come inside?' she replied with cool dignity, giving way to Skye's silent demand while exerting her own pressure for a private meeting.

'Of course,' Skye muttered, opening the gate and handing Matt the door-keys. 'Go ahead and change into play clothes while I see to business.'

Accustomed as he was to her dealing with clients, Matt didn't question the situation, and Skye breathed a sigh of relief when he obeyed without giving in to the temptation to question the lady about the extraordinary size of her car, either.

Skye watched him go inside before turning back to Luc's mother whose gaze was still trained on the opened front door which Matt had left ajar for them to follow. Inviting *the enemy* inside was certainly not to Skye's liking. She quickly asked, 'Why have you come here, Mrs Peretti?'

'I wanted to see my grandchild,' came the flat answer.

'You've seen him.'

'He's like Luciano.' The words were wistful, with an undercurrent of yearning.

'And me,' Skye stated fiercely, demanding her parenthood be recognised.

Luc's mother heaved a weary sigh as she returned her gaze to Skye. 'I knew nothing of how you and the child were dealt with until my husband informed me of it last Easter.'

'You didn't want me for Luc any more than your husband did,' Skye threw at her, certain it was true.

Flavia Peretti nodded. 'But Luciano will marry you nonetheless,' she said resignedly. 'He will not change his mind. For him it is a point of honour.'

'He loves me. And Matt,' Skye stated fiercely, resenting the implication that it was only honour driving Luc's desire to marry her. She did not believe it. Would not believe it.

'Do you love him?'

'Yes, I do. He's the only man I've ever loved. Ever will love. And I will not let you talk me out of marrying him, no matter what arguments you use, no matter what you might offer me, so your visit is a waste of your time and mine, Mrs Peretti.'

Skye's outburst seemed to make no impression on her. She bypassed it all, simply asking, 'When is the wedding date?'

'Soon.' Caution screamed not to name the day.

'Before Christmas?'

'It's none of your business, Mrs Peretti.'

'My son is getting married and it's none of my business?' It was a raw cry, scraped from a deep bank of emotion.

'You didn't care about what *he* wanted. You only care about what you want,' Skye retorted, fighting the possessiveness that had led to all her grief.

'I am Luciano's mother. As the mother of a son yourself…the only one I have left…'

Unbelievably, the haughty arrogance crumbled, tears welling into her eyes. And Skye couldn't help feeling sorry for her: this proud woman, weeping on a public street, this sad woman who had lost one son and was on the verge of losing the only one she had left. Regardless of the hurt she'd given in the past, she was Luc's mother, and Skye imagined her watching lovingly over Luc as a little boy, just as she did Matt.

It was impossible to leave her standing here like this. 'Come inside, Mrs Peretti,' Skye gently urged, taking her arm to steer her up the path and into the house.

Letting in the enemy.

Except it no longer felt like that.

Until she told Luc what had happened.

CHAPTER FOURTEEN

LUC'S call came through at seven o'clock that night, right on Matt's bedtime. Knowing this, he asked to speak to Matt first so he could say goodnight to him, and since Matt was jumping up and down in his eagerness to speak to his father, Skye passed the telephone receiver to him.

'Guess what, Daddy?' he cried excitedly. 'I met your Mummy today. She's my grandmother and she said to call her Nonna.'

He went on to describe the big black car this amazing new person in his life had come in, while Skye worried over how Luc was reacting to the news. She had strongly felt it would be wrong to gag Matt on the subject of his grandmother. It would have raised too many questions and none of the answers were appropriate for a little boy's understanding. Better to let him be happy about the relationship since there seemed to be a possibility that it could turn out good for him.

Matt prattled on, obviously prompted by questions Luc was putting to him about the meeting. His voice remained happy, signalling that Luc was carefully playing to their son's innocence. Skye hoped she had done the right thing with Flavia Peretti, but the difficult hump of past history was still playing on her mind. It was a relief when Matt finally said goodnight to his father and passed the receiver to her.

'Go on to bed now, Matt,' she instructed. 'You can read until I come in to say goodnight. Okay?'

'Okay, Mummy.' He shot her a proud grin. 'Nonna was surprised at how well I can read, wasn't she?'

Skye smiled back at him. 'Yes, she was. Off you go, Matt.'

She watched him skip out of the kitchen while she took a deep breath to ease her inner tension before speaking to Luc.

'Skye?' Urgency in his voice.

'Yes. I was just waiting for Matt to be out of ear-shot.'

'Tell me what happened.'

Skye recounted everything as best she could; the presence of the black limousine in their street for the past three afternoons, his mother's emergence from it today, the meeting on the sidewalk, her own stand about trying to keep the confrontation away from Matt, what was said and the reaction to it.

'My mother has a long habit of using tears to break down opposition and get her own way,' Luc commented tersely. 'She succeeded in getting you to let her meet Matt.'

Had it been deliberate manipulation? Skye hadn't thought so at the time. Surely it had been genuine distress. Besides, hadn't Luc himself said it would be her one and only grandchild who would bring his mother around?

'I thought you wanted her to, Luc.'

'Not like this, behind my back,' came the savage retort, making Skye cringe at having made a wrong judgement. Had she let in the enemy? Was this the thin edge of a wedge designed to drive her and Luc apart?

'I'm sorry. I…'

'No, I'm sorry,' he quickly cut in, tempering his tone. 'It's not your fault. I should have been expecting this, should have warned you.'

'Warned me of what?' Alarm tingled through every nerve in her body.

There was a long expulsion of breath at his end. 'Did my mother ask you to postpone our wedding?'

Giving his father time…to do what? How could anything be worse than what had been done to them six years ago? They were strong together now. Surely they could weather any attempt at interference.

'I didn't give her a date, Luc, but she did plead for us to wait until after Christmas. I said I'd have to discuss it with you.'

'Right! Why did she pinpoint Christmas?'

'She's offering Christmas Day as a day of reconciliation. For family mending.'

'Did you believe she meant it?'

Skye hesitated, but she had truly felt Flavia Peretti had spoken sincerely. 'Is there any reason why I shouldn't?' she asked warily. 'I thought you'd want this, Luc.'

'It depends on what it costs. What was her attitude towards you, Skye?'

'Stiff at first, but she wasn't…well, looking down her nose at me. It was more a kind of awkward acceptance. Her focus was more on Matt than on me, Luc. I think she truly wants Matt in her life and will do all she can to…to smooth things over.'

'There was nothing…offensive?'

'Not really. I don't expect a sudden flow of benevolence towards me from your mother. I never was what she wanted for you and I haven't miraculously changed into the perfect Italian bride. But I honestly felt she was making an effort today not to be disapproving of anything.'

'There's nothing to disapprove of,' he said fiercely, giving Skye the warm reassurance that he truly believed it and would fight to the death anyone who suggested otherwise.

It helped her relax, made her feel safe again. Luc was not being critical of her actions. He was being protective of her, angry that he had not been at her side to handle whatever was coming at her from his family.

'I don't like this…my mother visiting you behind my back,' he went on. 'Most probably behind my father's back, too. As if we haven't had enough deception messing us around!'

And they'd certainly both suffered from it. But giving suffering back did not right the wrong. Skye took a deep breath and tentatively suggested, 'She might have come as a go-between peace-maker.'

A harsh laugh. 'God knows! But I'll sure as hell find out before this goes any further. I've booked a four o'clock flight for tomorrow afternoon. Should be with you and Matt in time for dinner.'

'Do you want us to pick you up at the airport?'

'No. I'll catch a taxi, save the hassle. Don't worry about my mother's visit, Skye. I'll sort it out when I get home. Okay?'

She sighed, relieved to have this assurance, too.

'One thing,' he added in a determined tone. 'We

are not postponing our wedding for anything so don't even think about it. We love each other and we're going to get married on our agreed date.'

'That's good to hear,' she said, smiling over the fervour in his voice, though she was no longer sure it was a good idea to marry before Christmas. Flavia Peretti had raised issues that had made her feel very selfish about maintaining her small safe world with Luc.

'I'll let you go and tend to Matt now,' he said in a softer tone. 'Be with you soon.'

'Yes. 'Bye for now.'

'Love you.'

'Me, too.'

She did love him. But she was beginning to realise how much Luc's commitment to her was costing him and how blind she had been to that, only seeing that his family circle could hurt her. And Matt. It still could, but if she believed enough in Luc's love for her, wasn't there room for giving some kind of reconciliation a trial?

Watching his mother with Matt this afternoon…it had made her wish her own mother was still alive, taking pleasure in the grandchild she'd only known as a baby. Death was something no one could control—a final parting from which there was no turning back. Flavia Peretti had experienced that with Roberto. But the separation from Luc could be bridged if the prejudice against a non-Italian bride was set aside, and the pride of Luc and his father did not remain an ongoing battle-ground.

Big *ifs*.

And Skye knew she was right at the centre of them.

Moving from her own stance on Luc's family was absolutely essential if a truce was to be called. The big question was…and her heart quailed at facing it…how was she going to cope if she was continually made to feel not good enough for Luc? Good intentions could be very quickly undermined.

She had a bad night.

The next day wasn't much better, her tired mind still fretting over what should be done. At least every hour that dragged by was one hour less of being alone with her dilemma. It was a huge relief when Luc finally arrived home and wrapped her in his strong embrace, making her feel warm and secure in his love.

Matt, of course, was still full of his new Nonna over dinner, questioning Luc incessantly about his life as a child, learning that he'd had a younger brother and immediately deciding he'd like a brother, too. Which made Luc smile and cock a quizzical eyebrow at Skye.

'Maybe in another year or two, Matt,' she said, knowing Luc wanted at least one more child—one whose life he would be aware of right from the beginning, no missing out on anything. 'But your Daddy and I can't guarantee a brother. It might be a sister instead,' she cautioned.

'Oh!' He thought about it. 'That's all right, Mummy. I like girls, too.'

And no doubt they liked him, Skye thought. He *was* like Luc in lots of ways. Which made her feel all the more guilty about depriving Flavia Peretti of her grandchild, as well as her Luciano. She was glad when Matt's bedtime came and he was finally tucked in for the night, giving her and Luc the privacy needed to discuss the situation.

Luc wanted to sweep her off to bed but her need to talk first was paramount in Skye's mind, so she insisted they sit over coffee at the kitchen table. Which was not to his liking. His dark frown and suspicious eyes drove an instant flutter of apprehension through her heart.

'You're letting my mother's visit affect what we'd normally do,' he growled.

She looked at him in eloquent appeal. 'I can't discount it, Luc. Please?'

She made coffee and they sat, but the aggressive energy pouring from him made it difficult for Skye to know where to start. She felt Luc was going to pounce on anything she said and tear it apart. Did the harmony in their relationship depend on having no contact with his family? Or was this all her fault for making such a huge issue of it? It was impossible to forget the scars of the past, but weren't she and Luc strong enough together now to rise above them?

'My own mother is gone, Luc,' she began nervously. 'On my side there's no family, and no closely connected community forming an extension of family, either. There's only me and Matt.'

'And me,' Luc shot at her grimly.

'I'm not doubting that, Luc,' she hastily assured him.

'You're drawing lines, Skye.'

It forced her to choose her words more carefully. 'I just meant…you still have…other people who care about you.'

'Not so I've noticed,' he snapped, his face growing harder, his eyes angry.

'Because I haven't given you the chance to be with them,' she rushed out. 'I've been a coward, not facing up to your life, wanting to be safe in my own little world.'

'You have every right to want to feel safe,' he fiercely argued. 'As for chances, my father could have chosen any amount of chances to invite us into his home.'

Skye took a deep breath. 'Well, there might be a chance now.'

'According to my mother?' he flashed at her with deep scepticism. 'Along with her request to postpone our wedding? Can't you see she's dangling out an acceptance of you to stop what she and my father want to stop?'

'They can't stop us from getting married if we don't let them, Luc. I trust you on that. Can't you trust me?'

'It's taken me so long to convince you it's right for us…'

'And it is. I know it is. But I'm now feeling wrong about the way we're doing it.'

His jaw clenched. Skye sensed he was about to erupt from his chair, but the moment of shimmering violence passed. 'Why?' he bit out.

She shook her head over the realisation that her fears had driven Luc to an extreme stand, and he was not prepared to back down from it. He hadn't spelled out that in marrying her without his parents' blessing, he'd make himself an exile, but she had blindly accepted that sacrifice from him, accepted taking him away from others, too. She'd actually been intensely relieved that she didn't have to worry about *them* any more. Selfish relief.

'Your mother loves you, Luc,' she said quietly.

His head jerked aside as though he didn't want to be hit by that. He grimaced and turned his gaze back to her, eyes blazing with resolution. 'I won't have you hurt again, Skye. In all but law you're my wife now. My first allegiance is to you.'

She took another deep breath and said, 'Your parents didn't know how deeply you felt about me. They made a mistake.'

'That's putting it kindly,' he mocked, still not giving an inch.

'I'm not saying this to test you, Luc. I've thought about nothing else since your mother came.' She tried a smile to lighten the tension. 'As you just said, I'm your wife now in everything but the legality. Does it really matter if we postpone going to a registry office until after Christmas?'

His responding smile carried a load of irony. 'Did my mother promise you a big Italian wedding if we did?'

'No, she didn't.'

'Did she say if you loved me, you'd ensure that I come home for Christmas Day for the sake of family feeling?'

She sighed, regretting the huge barriers she had built. 'It wasn't like that, Luc. Your mother was very distressed at the rift that has developed. Can't you just accept that without colouring it as more deception?'

'And if it is deception?' he bored in.

'We'll know soon enough, won't we? Christmas is only five weeks away.'

'Don't count on my mother's peace-plan going through. I doubt my father knows about it. And I will not be going to Bellevue Hill again without his personal invitation.'

This was said with so much harsh pride, it made Skye wonder how much Luc himself had contributed to the rift. Her reaction to the deception with the photos and her acute awareness of being considered an undesirable in the Peretti family circle had certainly played its part. Given Luc's reaction to what she was saying now, perhaps he had drawn battle-lines with his father that couldn't be crossed by either side.

'He is your father, Luc,' she reminded him.

'No father has the right to do what he did.'

The vehemence in his voice left no room for argument. Besides which, what he said was true. His father had abrogated Luc's right to choose whether to know or deny his own child. It was a monstrous thing to do.

'What about your mother, then?' she asked. 'Must she pay for your father's decisions? She didn't know, Luc. She didn't know until Easter, when you didn't turn up for Easter Sunday.'

'But she doesn't turn up until now, trying to put off our wedding,' he pointed out, no softening at all in his expression.

It's gone too far, Skye thought, feeling totally miserable about it. 'I said she could come again, Luc,' she confessed on a heavy sigh. 'Matt was so excited about having a grandmother...'

'It's okay. Stop worrying about it, Skye.'

He was on his feet, coming around the table to her. She felt too drained to move, too torn by the conflicts that still raged around them to achieve any peace of mind. Luc stepped behind her chair and his hands slid over her shoulders and started a gentle massage.

'None of this is your fault,' he murmured, dropping a kiss on the top of her head, caring for her uppermost in his tone now. 'Try to relax, Skye. If my mother visits again…just let it be. Matt is her grandson. So long as the connection is good for him, no harm done.'

The tension in her shoulders eased under his expert manipulation. 'What about you, Luc? You're her son.'

'I'll welcome her if I'm with you and Matt. But don't be surprised if she never comes again. My father might forbid it. In which case…'

'Forbid?' She shook her head over the harsh concept.

'It's an old-fashioned Italian marriage,' Luc said wryly. 'Love, honour, obey…'

'Is that how you think, too? That you have the right to forbid me to do something you disapprove of?'

'No. I don't own you, Skye. I don't see marriage as a form of ownership. Nor do I see parenthood that way. There comes a time when you have to let a child choose his own path, even against what you think are his best interests.'

'What if your father honestly thought how he acted was in your best interests, Luc?'

'It doesn't excuse hurting you as he did.'

'He didn't know me.'

Caring too much about one person could make you

blind to others, Skye thought. And protecting the life you know can make you blind to others' lives, too. It was what she'd been doing.

Luc's thumbs pressed harder into her muscles as he said, 'He didn't *try* to know you.'

Anger again.

Anger built on her anger at what had been done to her. Perhaps anger at himself, as well, for believing what he should never have believed, knowing her as intimately as he had. But that was far in the past now, and Skye didn't want their future built on such a divisive foundation.

'What if he tries now, Luc?'

The movement of his hands halted. He dragged in a deep breath and exhaled it very slowly. 'Let's not talk about my father, Skye. It's you I need.'

The raw need in his voice compelled her to rise from her chair and give him whatever he wanted of her. He instantly caught her to him, one arm sweeping around her waist, one hand lifting to her face to stroke away any worry lines. His eyes searched hers with a searing intensity.

'I love you. Don't let anything come between us.'

The passionate plea carried the scars of their past experience, and Skye knew intuitively they'd been brought to throbbing life again by the intrusion of his family. She curled her arms around his neck and kissed him, not wanting him to feel any uncertainty about her love. That was strong and true, always had been, always would be.

They went to bed and made love long into the night.

Skye did not doubt Luc's commitment to her for a second.

But not even the secure comfort of being this close to him could banish the sense of wrongs which still had to be righted.

CHAPTER FIFTEEN

'PLEASE...sit with me.'

Flavia Peretti gestured to the two deck chairs on the small back verandah where Matt had led his Nonna to watch him kick the soccer ball around the backyard. Skye had hurried out to check there was no bird's mess on either of them before Luc's mother sat down. She had meant to leave her with her grandson, but it seemed too impolite to refuse such a direct request.

She sat, the old deck chair creaking as she did so, making her conscious of the huge difference between her living circumstances and that of the Peretti family. Everything about the cottage was old and shabby—she couldn't afford better—though she'd brightened it up with colour where she could. Here on the verandah, the petunias she'd potted were in full bloom, looking very pretty. A cheap little garden, Skye thought, but one that gave her pleasure.

Oddly enough, in her three visits to the cottage, Luc's mother had made no disdainful comment on Skye's relatively poor circumstances. Nor did she now.

'Matteo is a credit to you, Skye.'

Spoken with warm approval.

And actually using her first name.

Which made two firsts.

It was Flavia Peretti's third visit and she was finally

148

thawing from polite formality. Skye smiled. She didn't mind basking in her son's reflected glory. It was clearly difficult for Luc's mother to release the prejudice she had held against her son's non-Italian girlfriend and see the woman he loved.

'My husband…' Flavia gathered herself to look directly at Skye, a sad plea in her eloquent dark eyes. 'He says my invitation for Christmas Day is enough. If Luciano won't come, bringing you and our grandson, for my sake…' She gestured helplessly.

'I'm sorry, Mrs Peretti.'

'No…no…you have nothing to apologise for. It is we who must make up for what was done. But Maurizio…he has his pride. The father does not go to the son, you understand.'

'I can't say I do understand,' Skye said ruefully.

'You are not steeped in our traditions.' A deep sigh was heaved. 'Our marriage was an arranged one by our two families. That was how it was done. Maurizio came back to Italy for me and I came to Australia with him as his bride. He has been a good husband. And as a good father, he believed he was doing right by Luciano.'

Skye shook her head, seeing nothing right in what had been done to Luc and herself.

Flavia Peretti grimaced apologetically and rushed out an explanation. 'He did not understand the attachment to you. How could it be so when you were not one of us? To Maurizio it was a bad distraction from what should be Luciano's duty to the family. He asked Roberto to help and it was done. You were gone.'

'It was a terrible thing to do, Mrs Peretti,' Skye put in quietly.

'You were…a modern Australian girl. And—' she shrugged '—not a virgin.'

A heated protest sprang to Skye's lips. 'That doesn't make me a woman who jumps into any man's bed. I have only ever been with Luc.'

'Please…' Hands were raised in anguished appeal. 'I did not mean to insult you. I was trying to explain why it did not seem so terrible to Maurizio. When he learned of your pregnancy, he did make generous provision for the child so you would never be in need. In his mind, Luciano should understand all these things.'

The clash of cultures, Skye thought, wondering if there was any real chance of finding any meeting ground.

'A son should forgive his father a mistake which was made with his good at heart,' was the next pleading argument. 'Can you not speak to Luciano about this?'

'Why don't you speak to him yourself, Mrs Peretti?'

A weary roll of her eyes. 'He is a man. If anyone can get past his pride, it will be you, the woman he loves, the woman for whom he is turning his back on his family.'

This last statement hit Skye hard.

Luc would undoubtedly call it emotional blackmail, yet there was too much truth in it for her to dismiss it out of hand. In the end, family was family and the blood connection ran deep. It didn't go away, not even if one turned one's back on it. The memories were always there.

*   *   *

As Luc drove his Ferrari into Skye's street, a black limousine was turning the corner at the other end of the block.

His mother!

This was the third time she'd come without making any contact with him!

He put his foot on the accelerator in a burst of frustration, instinctively responding to the urge to chase her down and demand she stop bothering Skye. Only the sure knowledge that a confrontation between them would not achieve anything made him think better of going in pursuit. He slowed the car and pulled it in beside the kerb, thumping the driving wheel in anger as he switched off the engine.

The agreed wedding day was set for one week away. It was pointless to put it off until after Christmas. His father was never going to come around to accepting their marriage. He had made no attempt to arrange a private meeting with Luc at work. A reconciliation on Christmas day was definitely not on *his* drawing board.

And here was his mother meddling again!

Sure she probably wanted to see Matt—he was a wonderful grandchild for her—but it was Skye she was getting at, planting whatever seeds of dissension she could. Luc felt the difference each time she'd been; worries, tension, questions when there shouldn't be any questions.

Today had been Matt's last day at school for the year. As Luc alighted from his car, that time factor eased some of his own tension. There was no longer any need for Skye and Matt to stay at this house in

Brighton-Le-Sands. No excuse not to come and live with him at Bondi. Next year another school could be found for Matt, close to wherever they bought a suitable home—certainly a lot more suitable than this cheap little rental cottage where Skye had insisted on staying all year, clinging to her independence.

Which might well have given his mother hope that Skye wasn't completely committed to the marriage!

Luc strode across the street, setting his mind on a plan of action. He was not going to lose Skye now. No way. In fact, he'd help her start on packing her belongings tonight, sorting out what she wanted to keep and what could be given away to charity. Best to make the move to his apartment this weekend. That might stop his mother from sneaking visits behind his back.

He used the front door key Skye had given him and had no sooner stepped into the hallway than Matt came flying down it to meet him. 'Nonna was here again, Daddy. You've just missed her,' he cried, his happy face expecting Luc to feel both pleased and disappointed.

'Well, she should have timed her visit better,' he replied lightly, ruffling Matt's hair to project some fun into the moment. 'How was your last day at school?'

Skye was in the kitchen, cutting up vegetables for dinner. She smiled at him as he came in with Matt but there was a strained look in her lovely blue eyes and she didn't stop working to greet him beyond saying, 'Hi!' No hug. No kiss. A quick instruction to Matt. 'Let your father sit down and relax before you talk his head off.'

There was a tight restraint about her that knotted Luc's gut. He managed to drink the beer Matt brought him but it didn't relax him, and for once, his son's bright chatter did not give him joy. It took an act of will to respond to it. His gaze kept turning to Skye who just went ahead, preparing dinner, occasionally joining in the conversation, trying to act naturally as though nothing was wrong.

Luc wasn't fooled. However, it was impossible to say anything in front of Matt. Their son was a complete innocent in all of this, and should be kept so, unless circumstances forced knowledge on him that had to be dealt with. Luc had the feeling those circumstances were gathering around them very ominously at the moment.

He silently railed against his father's stubborn refusal to accept the woman he loved. Skye was everything he could possibly want in a wife. She had so many admirable attributes, far beyond her outer beauty. Was his mother seeing that now? Was she plotting to stop the marriage or was she beginning to recognise Skye's qualities?

Matt was still enthusiastic about his Nonna so there couldn't have been any unpleasantness between his new grandmother and his mother. Not in front of him. Yet something was seriously disturbing Skye. Luc could sense the anxiety behind her every look at him.

He forced restraint on himself all through dinner and the cleaning up afterwards. As soon as they'd bade Matt goodnight and switched the light off in his bedroom, Luc drew Skye straight into hers, closing the door behind them, wanting to close the door on anything that might separate them. He wrapped her in his arms, kissing her with all the deep passion she evoked in him, relief heightening his need for her as he felt her uninhibited response.

This, at least, was right.

It had always been right.

And she was as eager to strip off his clothes as he was to get rid of hers. He loved her. He took her to bed, determined on showing her how utterly and completely he did. She was so incredibly beautiful; the silky softness of her long glorious hair, the lush curves of her that were all woman, the smooth litheness of her legs, winding so possessively around him as he revelled in the sweet fire of her sexuality, knowing she was craving his.

He drove her through climax after climax, controlling his own excitement until it reached breaking point, bursting with the need to melt into her, be one with her, the ultimate sharing of themselves. Her sigh of fulfilment told him she was with him all the way and he kissed her to feel it even more intensely, to feel nothing could ever separate them. They belonged together, as deeply as any man and woman could.

The sense of blissful harmony carried over into their lying together afterwards, Skye's head resting contentedly over his heart as he leisurely caressed her back. 'I want to move you and Matt to my place this weekend,' he murmured. 'There's no reason for you to stay here any more, Skye, and I want you settled with me.'

'Yes,' she agreed, her warm breath fanning his skin, giving pleasure as her answer gave him pleasure.

Luc felt secure enough now to casually probe the concerns his mother's visit had raised. 'What's troubling you, Skye? Did my mother push again for us to postpone our marriage?'

She didn't lift her head. Her hand glided down to stroke the erotic area under his hipbone as she spoke. 'Those legal papers we signed…they're good for three months, Luc. We don't have to get married on the date we set.'

The delightful fuzz of sensual pleasure was instantly ripped from his mind. He grabbed her hand, squeezing it so hard she cried out his name in protest. But he was already rolling, slamming her hand into the pillow as her head came to rest on it, his heart pumping a much louder protest at what she was allowing to happen, what she was aiding and abetting.

'You asked me if I'd walk away from everything for you and Matt. I have,' he fiercely declared, seething over her inconstancy. 'Don't backtrack on me now, Skye. It's done. If you don't keep your word to me…'

'Luc, I will marry you. I will.' Alarm in her eyes. 'And I'll go with you wherever you choose to go. That's not in question.'

'Oh, yes it is.' Blood was pounding through his head with the urgent need to make her see what she was doing. 'You're actively betraying my love for you by listening to my mother, letting yourself be drawn into giving consideration to people who hurt you. Who will hurt you again. And do everything they can to take you from me.'

'They won't, Luc. I promise you. Nothing can tear me away from you now,' she said earnestly. 'But I shouldn't have asked you to give up everything, to sacrifice—'

'It's no sacrifice. It's freedom. Throwing off the shackles of an ownership I now refute in all its malevolent forms. I will not have it touch us.'

'Malevolent…' She repeated the word as though it tormented her. 'I made it so, Luc.'

'No.'

'What if it isn't?'

'My God!' he cried in exasperation. 'What more proof do you need? How can you forget what was done to us?'

'Your mother—'

'My mother has her own agenda. My father has not said one word to me about Christmas Day. Nothing is going to change in that court, believe me.'

'Please—' she sucked in a deep breath, her eyes searching his in frantic appeal '—will you just listen to me?'

He gritted his teeth, hating the fact there could be any issue about this.

'Please,' she begged.

He couldn't bear watching the damage already wrought by his mother's insidious visits. Yet to forbid Skye to give voice to it put him in the same frame his father occupied—the all too dominating male, leaning over her, leaning *on* her. He flung himself onto his back. Lying beside her was less threatening, giving her space to express what he didn't want to hear. His whole body was still keyed up to attack and forcing restraint was not easy.

'I'm listening,' he bit out.

She heaved a deep sigh. He could feel her distress

at his abrupt separation from her, but he couldn't bring himself to soothe it. Skye had to realise a wedge was being driven between them.

'Did you know your parents' marriage had been arranged by their families, Luc?'

His hands clenched at this harking back to a past which had nothing to do with them. 'What *they* accepted then—'

'Has a bearing on what was done to us, Luc,' she rushed out, rolling onto her side, propping herself up on one elbow, reaching out to lay her hand on his chest, softly stroking as though trying to soothe the savage beast in him.

He said nothing.

If she needed him to listen, he'd listen. And he did listen, trying to understand how she could forgive his father enough to even consider the prospect of a meeting with him, let alone tolerate it, especially when there was not one suggestion of an apology coming for what he'd done to her.

Her guilt over separating him from his family was absurd. She had done nothing to deserve their rejection. The fault lay entirely with his parents' prejudiced attitudes. *They* had to make the change.

This was Australia, not Italy, and they had made their lives here where the customs were different. If they couldn't face up to the difference—a difference Luc had grown up with, which was part and parcel of *his* thinking, then let them cling to their past and lose the future he and Skye could provide!

'I want you to go to your father, Luc.'

He closed his eyes. This was madness. For her to meet his father at all would be like walking into the lion's den, asking to be mauled. He couldn't let her do it. She had more than enough bad memories about his family. Adding freshly to them, connecting him to them…he didn't want to risk that.

'I've already been to him once,' he grated out.

'That was to tell him we were getting married.'

'And we are,' he stated determinedly.

She moved, lowering her body onto his, the softness of her breasts pressing into his chest, her arms burrowing under his neck, her warm breath tingling on his grimly tightened mouth. 'I love you,' she said with quiet fervour. 'And I'll marry you, no matter what.'

He opened his eyes. His hands slid over her back, up into her hair. An anguished wave of possessiveness swept through him. If they could just lose themselves in each other, make all these unnecessary issues go away…

'I'd just like to feel that everything's been done to…to mend fences, Luc.'

'They aren't our fences to mend, Skye,' he asserted, wanting her to turn aside from them, stay where she was safe. Where they were both safe.

'Does it matter if the move comes from you instead of your father?'

Yes, it mattered.

Her eyes probed his with a pleading intensity, wanting to find the giving that she was willing to give, yet everything in Luc resisted it. The giving should come from his father. Any softening from him would be interpreted as weakness, making them both vulnerable to attack.

'He hurt both of us very badly, Luc, but it was in not understanding the people we are,' she said softly.

'I'm his own son,' he bit out.

'And he thought you should be like him. You're not. Show him you're not by not being as rigid as he is.'

'He'll see it as crawling back to him, wanting what he can offer,' he argued in terse dismissal of the idea.

'*We* know it's not, Luc. It takes more strength to step over a battle-line and hold out a hand in peace than it does to keep fighting. If he doesn't meet you halfway, then I'll marry you whenever you want. But if he does...can we wait until after Christmas Day?'

He could see she wasn't going to let go of this idea. It would remain brooding in her mind if he refused to do what she asked, and perhaps he'd be the lesser man for it in her eyes.

He quelled the fierce rebellion in his heart. It went totally against his grain to go cap in hand for his father's blessing on a union which that same father had done his utmost to destroy. Even more critically, if a truce did eventuate, it gave his father the opportunity to undermine Skye's sense of security with him.

Nevertheless, if peace of mind on this issue was needed for them to achieve a happy future together, he had to take at least one step towards a reconciliation.

If his father turned away from it...no more!

He reached up to stroke the anxious line from between her brows. 'I'll speak to him about Christmas Day. Okay? If there's a positive response from him...'

She smiled. It was like sunlight bursting through clouds and his heart turned over. He didn't know how she could be so forgiving of the past. He knew only how much he loved her.

It was the last board meeting before Christmas. Luc watched his father work it with his usual commanding authority while treating his executives with the respect they deserved. As always it was an impressive performance, not missing a beat anywhere. If he was at all disturbed by personal family issues, it certainly didn't show.

Refreshments were wheeled in, along with bottles of champagne to toast another successful and highly profitable year for the Peretti Corporation. A festive mood took over, everyone happy to relax and socialise, the big boss playing the genial host to the hilt.

Luc wanted to walk out, turn his back on the whole scene. He'd done his job, given his end of year report, and he fiercely resented his father's bonhomie which telegraphed perfect peace of mind, while Skye fretted over an estrangement that *she* thought she'd caused. The irony was sickening.

Only his promise to her kept him there. He waited, circulating with every air of confidence himself, until most of the food had been eaten and the champagne bottles were empty. When he judged his father had done all the usual shoulder-clapping, he moved in with steely resolve.

'Could I have a private word with you, Dad?'

'Of course, Luciano,' he said genially, excusing himself from the group still gathered around him.

Luc followed him into the executive office adjoining the boardroom and closed the door, remaining beside it as his father moved around behind his desk, apparently intending to sit down.

'This won't take long,' Luc warned, hating the sense that he was in the position of a beggar.

His father paused beside his chair, seeming to gather himself before meeting Luc's hard gaze. He gestured open-handedly. 'I have as much time as you want.'

On his terms, Luc thought, but he tempered his tone to a less harsh note. 'You know Mamma has been visiting Skye and Matt?'

'Yes, I know.'

No other comment. Not a hint of approval or disapproval. Just a flat stare at Luc, waiting for him to make what he would of it.

'She extended an invitation for the three of us to join you on Christmas Day,' he threw at his father.

'Your mother is free to invite anyone she wishes,' came straight back at him.

Frustrated by the lack of any personal response, Luc bluntly asked, 'Where do you stand, Dad?'

His chin lifted in aggressive pride. 'Beside your mother. Where I have always stood.'

Again no personal comment on the invitation.

Luc studied his father's face, the whole indomitable demeanour of the man, and knew this was as good as he was going to get—a tacit acceptance, but no welcome mat rolled out and no apology for transgressions, either. He realised that for his father, that would be completely losing face, too humiliating. Yet there was something in his eyes…an intensity of feeling that was not pride.

Maybe it was a reaching out, or a wish to reach back to the time when his elder son had looked up to him. It struck a chord of sadness in Luc. He, too, wished for something different.

'We'll come,' he said. 'And I'll be standing beside Skye.'

It was both a challenge and a chance.

A great deal depended on how his father met it.

'I'll tell your mother,' he said, implicitly demanding trust.

Luc stared back at him, loath to give that trust without assurances. If Skye or Matt was abused in any way…

'Flavia is very taken with…our grandson,' his father stiffly added.

Our, not *her.*

A few more words were offered. 'I'm sure she will put some gifts for him under our Christmas tree.'

It was a start. The first concession. Luc didn't press for more. 'Christmas *is* for children,' he said, then nodded and left, telling himself at least Matt would be treated well. And Skye would risk it, since she was determined on trying to make peace with his family.

But be damned if he was going to stand by and see her hurt again!

CHAPTER SIXTEEN

CHRISTMAS Day…

Skye carefully attached the sapphire and diamond earrings to her lobes—Luc's Christmas gift to her. They matched the engagement ring he'd put on her finger when she'd finally agreed to marry him. There would have been a wedding ring already complementing it, but for the need she had to give Luc back his family.

She had no illusions about where she stood with his father and it was nerve-wracking having to face him today. But if Maurizio Peretti could tolerate her for the sake of having his son in the family fold again—and his grandson—she would somehow make herself tolerate him.

Besides, she knew Flavia Peretti would be working hard to smooth everything over. It was weird to think she and Luc's mother had become allies. Not friends. Friendship took a lot longer and might never eventuate. But it was good for Matt to have a grandmother who loved him.

Skye tucked the long fall of her hair behind her ear so at least one of the earrings showed, then stepped back to view her appearance in the mirror. She'd bought this dress especially for today, wanting to correct the impression she'd obviously given Luc's parents in the past when she'd worn more casual, form-fitting, *sexy* clothes—the in fashion—not realising she might be offending their sensibilities and possibly giving rise to the idea of her being a 'loose' woman.

The white linen shift was printed with turquoise and royal blue flowers with chartreuse leaves. The colour combination suited her very well, bringing out the blue in her eyes and contrasting nicely with the golden honey tan she had acquired since coming to live with Luc at Bondi Beach. The dress was sleeveless, befitting a hot summer day—which it was—the high scooped neckline was demure, and the simple style skimmed her figure rather than accentuating it.

Since rent for the Brighton-Le-Sands cottage no longer had to be paid and there was spare money to spend, she'd splashed out on turquoise sandals, as well, all in all making quite an elegant outfit, Skye thought. Her long blonde hair was smooth and shiny, her make-up minimal, and she couldn't see what else could have been done to make herself more presentable.

Luc's footsteps coming up the stairs of his two storey apartment alerted her to time going by, but a quick glance at her watch showed there was still a quarter of an hour before they had to leave for Bellevue Hill. Flavia Peretti had suggested a ten o'clock arrival, time for Matt to open gifts before morning tea.

Morning tea…

Nerves fluttered in Skye's stomach. Everything was bound to be terribly formal, not like the casual breakfast they'd had this morning with Matt too excited about his presents to sit at a table. They'd lounged around in Luc's lovely living room, eating raisin toast, sharing the fun of a beautiful Christmas morning together. Skye could only hope that what should be a joyful day remained so for Matt.

She turned around to face Luc as he entered their bedroom. 'Will I do?' she asked anxiously, thinking how perfect he looked in smartly tailored grey pants and a conservative white cotton shirt—acceptable anywhere and the light colours throwing up the striking attraction of his Italian heritage.

His dark eyes simmered with more than appreciation as they swept her from head to foot and back again. 'You look beautiful.'

'Luc, I was trying for respectable,' she appealed, feeling her skin flush under the heat of his appraisal and becoming unsure of her choice. Was it too colourful, too cheap-looking?

His expression instantly changed to thunderous. 'You don't have to prove anything to my parents, Skye. Absolutely nothing! If they don't…'

She moved quickly to place her hand over his lips, stopping the burst of angst. 'I want to look right for Christmas at their home, Luc. Just tell me if I do or don't.'

His breath hissed out from between clenched teeth. 'If it's making you feel like this, we shouldn't be doing it.'

She moved her hand to the tight muscles in his jaw, resting it there lovingly as she spoke a truth they had not discussed for a long time. 'When you saw the photographs of Roberto and the woman pretending to be me, you believed them, Luc. You believed what your father thought of me.'

'Skye…' It was a groan of pain, tortured regret in his eyes.

'Maybe part of it was my going to bed with you too easily, giving in to the desire we felt. And maybe part of it was the kind of clothes I wore, the wrong image for—' she grimaced at the term as she delivered it '—for a good girl.'

'Skye, I have wished a thousand times that I had believed you and not Roberto. I can't undo that...'

'It doesn't matter any more, Luc. It stopped mattering when you convinced me you really did love me this time around. And I'll never bring it up again.'

His arms swept around her, drawing her into a possessive embrace as his eyes begged her belief. 'You mean more to me than anything else.'

'I know. I know,' she repeated to assure him there were no doubts about his love in her mind. 'You walked away from your family, for my sake. I'll never forget you did that. But if I let this rift go on, you'll all be suffering a far greater loss than I did. A much longer loss. And that's not fair, Luc. Mistakes were made on both sides and I want to correct mine.'

He shook his head, still pained by her insecurities. 'You were just you, Skye.'

'I didn't know any better then.' She gave him an ironic smile, trying to lessen his concern for her. 'I'm older and wiser now and it doesn't hurt me to dress as appropriately as I can to please your parents on such an occasion as this. I'd like them to look at me and think...well, I won't completely shame them as their daughter-in-law.'

'They should be proud to own you as one of the family,' he asserted earnestly.

'I think that will take time. I'm not expecting much

today. You shouldn't, either. I think we should both be very diplomatic.'

He grimaced, but the tense expression left his eyes, giving way to a wry admiration. 'You are an incredibly giving woman, Skye Sumner. And you do... beautifully. No one could possibly object to your appearance today. Not by any standard,' he fervently assured her.

She took a deep breath to calm her nerves and smiled her sunniest smile. 'Then I'm ready to go. Is Matt okay?'

'Happily sorting out the edges and corners for the *Harry Potter* jigsaw we're going to do together. I guess we'd better go and collect him.'

Twenty minutes later, Luc turned the red Alfa through a huge iron gateway and headed up a semi-circular drive, past perfectly manicured lawns and gardens to an incredibly large and imposing sandstone mansion.

'It's as big as a castle, Daddy,' Matt remarked in awe.

Was Maurizio Peretti going to be a gracious king, or a giant ogre, Skye wondered, trying desperately not to feel intimidated. Matt felt no fear at all. Once out of the car, he bounded up the front steps, eager to explore his Nonna's home, and when a formally dressed butler opened the door, Matt looked him up and down and promptly asked, 'Are you my grandfather?'

'No, Matt. This is Kirkwood, who's in charge of the house,' Luc quickly introduced.

'It's a very big house, Kirkwood,' Matt said, showing his awe.

The butler unbent enough to smile. 'Indeed, it is, young sir.'

Skye instantly started worrying about Matt's clothes. She'd dressed *young sir* in dark blue shorts and a turquoise shirt printed with white sailing boats, navy sandals on his feet. He looked gorgeous—a perfect little boy outfit, she'd thought when she'd bought it for him—but perhaps she should have chosen something more formal, more in keeping with being the grandson of Maurizio Peretti.

They were ushered into a large drawing room furnished with elegant antiques and currently dominated by the most magnificent Christmas tree Skye had ever seen—a silvery-blue tree which matched the furnishings, well over two metres high, and covered with exquisite ornaments.

Maurizio Peretti was standing in front of a marble fireplace, imposingly attired in a dark grey suit, a red silk tie possibly adding a festive touch. Flavia Peretti rose from a nearby sofa, and amazingly she wasn't wearing black today. Her dark red dress made her look younger, as did the smile she bestowed on Matt as he rushed forward to greet her.

'Nonna! Your Christmas tree is beautiful!'

He put so much expression into *beautiful,* she actually laughed. 'I'm glad you like it, Matteo.'

'I brought this for you,' he proudly handed her his gift which Skye had wrapped up for him in gold paper and tied with red ribbon. 'Happy Christmas, Nonna! It's a picture I drew of the beach where Daddy lives.'

No holding back by Matt! He hadn't yet learnt how to contain himself.

'Thank you, Matteo. Now come and meet your

grandfather.' She took his hand to lead him over to her husband whose gaze had been exclusively trained on the little boy, not lifting to acknowledge Luc and Skye. 'You call him Nonno,' Flavia instructed.

Skye couldn't help tensing and Luc's hand squeezed hers so hard she knew if his father did not respond reasonably to their son, Christmas Day at Bellevue Hill would be over before it had barely begun.

Matt looked up at his formidable grandfather and without so much as a pause, brightly said, 'Hello, Nonno. I brought you a gift, too. Happy Christmas!'

He held out his offering and Maurizio Peretti's hand slowly reached out and took it. 'Thank you.' It was a gravelled rumble from his throat, which he then cleared. 'Is it another picture you drew?'

Matt nodded. 'It's me playing soccer.'

'Ah! Your father told me you'd kicked more goals than anyone else in your team.'

'Thirty-two,' Matt told him proudly. 'And I got a trophy for it, Nonno.'

'Well done!'—said with hearty approval. He opened the gift, unrolled the drawing and a smile gradually softened his hard face as Matt explained all the action in it to him. 'I shall have this framed and put on my desk at work, Matteo. Everyone who comes in will see what a clever grandson I have.'

Public acceptance!

Skye breathed a sigh of relief.

Luc's fingers relaxed.

His father gave them both a cursory glance as he tossed a greeting at them. 'Happy Christmas! Come and sit down.' He waved to a sofa, then fastened his attention on Matt again. 'Underneath that beautiful tree, you might find some gifts for you. Why don't you go and have a look?'

The next hour passed peaceably enough with all of them focusing more on Matt's pleasure in his Christmas booty than on each other. Morning tea was served by the butler. Pressed into eating something by Flavia, Skye managed to get through a small mince pie and a sliver of rich fruit cake.

She was very conscious of Luc watching his father like a hawk, ready to pounce on any discourtesy to herself, but Maurizio Peretti skirted carefully around her, not once addressing her directly by name. She wasn't exactly ignored but there was definitely some resistance to her presence, making her feel very much on edge.

What words were spoken between the men were few and far between, as well. As soon as the butler had cleared away the morning tea, Maurizio Peretti was on his feet, holding out his hand to Matt. 'Come and have a walk with me around the grounds. I'll show you the sailing boats in the harbour, and maybe we can find a good place for us to play cricket after lunch.'

A cricket set had been amongst the gifts and Matt was instantly up and grasping his grandfather's hand, eager to go along with his plan.

Luc rose to his feet, bristling with purpose. 'I'll come with you.'

'No, no…' His father waved him to sit down again. 'Let me get to know my grandson. Besides, your mother has plans she wants to put to you.'

Skye knew Luc wanted to challenge him over his

less than welcoming manner to her but she hoped his father might thaw more over lunch. 'Let them go, Luc,' she softly pleaded.

'Yes, we have much to talk about,' his mother leapt in anxiously.

Rather than raise an argument in front of Matt, he reluctantly conceded to the arrangement, resuming his seat beside Skye and seething with silent resentment as he watched his father take his son off for their walk. The moment the door was closed behind them he turned to his mother and flatly declared, 'I won't have Skye ignored, Mamma.'

'Your father is feeling awkward, Luciano,' she quickly excused. 'Give him time. It is not a feeling he is used to. Perhaps Matteo will ease him out of it.'

Luc shook his head in impatient frustration. 'Well, what is it you want to talk about, Mamma?'

Their wedding!

Flavia Peretti laid out a plan that had Skye's mind reeling at its grand scale. Firstly, she wanted Luc to bring Skye and Matt to the New Year's Day luncheon party which the Perettis held every year—a gathering of all their closest friends and associates. It could serve to introduce Skye as his fiancée and be turned into an engagement party, celebrating their forthcoming marriage.

Then the invitations to the wedding could be sent out—six weeks' notice was enough—and a suitable marquee could be hired and set up in the grounds to accommodate the hundreds of guests. She went on and on, covering every detail of a production designed to inform the whole Italian community that

Luc's bride was to be acknowledged as a welcome addition to the Peretti family.

'Has Dad approved of this plan?' Luc tersely asked.

'You know it must be so, Luciano,' his mother pleaded rather than replied.

'You've discussed it with him?' Luc bored in, refusing to take anything for granted.

'Yes, of course.'

'Mamma, he stole Skye from me once. If this putting her on public display is meant to make her feel less than she is…if its purpose is to alienate her from me…'

'I swear it is not, Luciano,' his mother cried in alarm.

Luc beetled a frown at her. 'I see no sign of Dad treating Skye with respect.'

'He will. He *will*,' came the insistent reply.

'This plan may be his way of making amends, Luc,' Skye murmured, though she quailed at the thought of being put under such a spotlight in front of people whom she didn't know, people who didn't know her, people who were bound to look askance at the woman who'd borne a child out of wedlock and was probably forcing this unsuitable marriage because of it.

'Then why isn't he offering it himself?' Luc queried, his eyes searching hers for the truth of how she felt. 'You can't want to do this, Skye.'

'If it means a happier outcome all around…' She looked to his mother for guidance, believing that Flavia understood the complexities of the situation far better than she did. 'Is it necessary, Mrs Peretti?'

'No, it's not,' Luc cut in vehemently. 'We can get

married as planned. Privately. No more postpone-
ments.'

'Luciano, please…' his mother begged. 'I will help
Skye all I can. Do everything. She need only be here
for you.'

'Don't put this on me!' he fiercely retorted. 'I'm
not asking it of Skye. And you have asked too much
of her already, Mamma.' He rose to his feet, too
pumped up with aggressive energy to remain seated.
His hands flew into furious gesticulation as he fired
more shots at his mother. 'All these months ignoring
her…and now you expect her to perform for you. It's
too much. We get married how we want to get married.'

Flavia Peretti turned imploring eyes to Skye.
'Please…it is a matter of family honour.'

'And where was honour when Matt was born?' Luc
hurled at her. '*My* son!'

'Luc!' Skye's sharp cry switched his attention back
to her but his eyes were still blazing with turbulent
emotion. She shook her head at him and dredged up
the courage to do what had to be done. 'No more. It
has to stop now. Matt loves having his Nonna. He's
taken to your father, too. Let it be, Luc. I'll do it—'
her smile was meant to appeal to his strong, protective
instincts '—if you'll hold my hand.'

A few fast strides and he was back on the sofa with
her, holding both her hands. 'You don't have to do
this.'

'It doesn't matter. We're getting married, aren't
we?'

'Yes, but…'

'Your mother said she'd help me.'

'As I would a daughter,' Flavia Peretti swiftly promised.

'You see? It will be all right.'

The storm passed, though it left an unease which both women worked at glossing over; Luc's mother asking for Skye's input on everything to do with the wedding, Skye saying she was happy to go along with whatever Flavia advised. At the end of the day, she and Luc would be married, and if what she agreed to won his parents' blessing, that was what she had set out to achieve for him.

'Skye will choose her own wedding dress,' Luc insisted at one point, glowering at both of them.

His mother instantly agreed. 'Of course, she must. She is the bride.'

The bride…

It was weird to be called that. Skye didn't feel like a bride. Being a mother to Matt, living with Luc, having suffered through all they had to be together…a wedding like this felt very unreal to her. She had no guests to invite, no father to give her away. To her this whole plan was simply a process to ensure Luc would not lose anything by marrying her. But… maybe she would feel like a bride on her wedding day.

Matt came racing in ahead of his grandfather, full of exciting news. 'Mummy, you should see. There's a swimming pool and a tennis court and lots of flowers you'd like. Not just in pots.'

Maurizio Peretti strolled into the drawing room and Skye smiled at him, hoping he would share her pleasure in his grandson's happy list of wonderful things. His gaze skated right past her to his wife who nodded, apparently in answer to some silent question. His mouth twitched into a grim little smile and the mocking look he turned to Skye—his first direct look at her—made her own smile falter and die.

'I take it you're happy with the wedding arrangements.'

'Yes,' she agreed, though his attitude was swiftly giving her second thoughts.

'I had no doubt you would be,' he said with arrogant cynicism. 'Having no family yourself, and seeing all we can offer here…'

The implication was so gross, Skye completely lost sight of the purpose that had brought her to this monstrous castle of money—blood money that had got rid of her and paid for Matt's exclusion from their lives.

All the most negative emotions she'd ever had about the Perettis churned through her, driving her to her feet, Matt's hand firmly grasped in hers. She heard her voice shaking with a fierce primitive passion that literally burst from her.

'I do have family, Mr Peretti. I have my son. And believe me, I'm perfectly happy to take him away from everything you have here. I only came for Luc. Because I love him. I love him…'

Luc was suddenly beside her, his arm around her shoulders, hugging her tight, and to her intense mortification, a gush of tears welled into her eyes.

'Maurizio, you have this wrong!' his wife wailed, rushing forward to grab his arm to press her own belief, shaking it in her angst. 'The cottage she lived in…she would not even take from Luciano!'

'Mamma, you waste your breath.' Luc growled. 'I'm taking Skye home.'

'No…no…' In panicking protest, his mother whirled past her husband to block their way, flapping her hands in distress. 'I don't want you to go. Maurizio, this is not right. You must see it is not.'

It was a horribly painful situation.

Skye could feel Luc's father glaring at her, hating the dissension she had brought to his household. Luc was holding her protectively. She was hanging on to Matt's hand, savagely possessive of him in her own distress. Flavia Peretti made it impossible for Luc to manoeuvre all three of them past her.

The wretched impasse pulsed with enormous stress. Into the dreadfully fraught silence came Matt's little boy voice, quavering with incomprehension and fright at what was going on around him, yet incredibly homing in on the heart of the problem.

'Nonno…why don't you love my Mummy?'

A hysterical bubble of laughter almost broke over the terrible lump in Skye's throat. *Love* her? Luc's father had hated her all along! It didn't matter what she did, however many concessions she made…

'Matt, we're just going to take your mother home,' Luc said firmly.

'But, Daddy…'

'I'll explain later, Matt. We must leave now. Mamma, if you'll just step aside…'

'No!' The emphatic command from Maurizio Peretti was followed up by his moving to stand by his wife, ensuring their departure was blocked. 'The boy has a right to ask,' he declared, challenging Luc before turning his gaze down to their son.

'Dad…' Luc threatening.

'Matteo…the reason why I do not love your mother

is because I do not know her. I have not taken the time to know her. And for that—' he lifted his gaze directly to Skye '—I apologise.'

Silence.

The apology might have been wrung from him but it was hanging out there to be accepted, completely confusing Skye. Was it sincere or…or what? He had certainly spoken the truth. He did not know her.

'You could get to know my Mummy now, Nonno,' Matt reasoned in his innocence. 'Daddy knows her real good and he loves her.'

'Yes, he does,' Maurizio Peretti conceded to Matt, then looked directly at Luc before adding. 'I know he does.'

Skye had no idea what passed between the two men. Her vision was hopelessly blurred, but she could feel the tension of absolute war slightly easing.

'Mummy likes flowers,' Matt informed helpfully. 'You could take her for a walk, Nonno, and show her your garden.'

'That sounds like a very good idea, Matteo. Perhaps after lunch, your mother would agree to accompany me. And I can apologise more fully for not knowing her.'

Matt tugged on her dress. 'Please don't cry, Mummy. Nonno didn't mean to upset you. He just didn't know.'

Skye brushed the wetness from her cheeks with the back of her hand, still too choked up to speak.

Maurizio Peretti cleared his throat. 'Skye…if I may call you that…'

'It's her name,' Luc fiercely muttered.

'Will you offer me...an olive branch...for the sake of those we love?'

It was why she had come.

Maybe the sentiment was genuine, maybe it wasn't.

She still had to try.

In her hands was the power to build a family or destroy one.

She swallowed hard, sucked in a deep breath, lifted her head to hold it high, and said, 'Yes, I will, Mr Peretti.'

'Bravo!' he murmured, and for the very first time, she saw a glint of admiration in Maurizio Peretti's eyes.

For her.

'What's an olive branch, Daddy?' Matt asked.

'It's the gift of love, Matt. Your mother is telling your grandfather how much she loves both of us. And I hope he understands it.'

'Do you, Nonno?'

'Yes, I do, Matteo.'

'Mummy could love you, too.'

'That, my dear child, would be a miracle, but since it's Christmas Day, miracles can happen.'

'Indeed, they can,' Flavia breathed in relief. Then quite briskly, 'Come, Matteo, we'll go and wash your hands before lunch. Maurizio, you'd best check the wine with Kirkwood.'

Which neatly left Luc and Skye alone to have some private time together. He turned her to face him, gently tilting her chin up to look into her eyes. 'Are you really okay with this, Skye?'

'No. Not yet. But I'll get there,' she answered shakily.

'You're determined on it?'

'So long as you hold my hand.'

'All my life,' he promised.

And she knew he would keep that promise, regardless of whatever happened today, tomorrow, next week, next month, next year, all their future together.

CHAPTER SEVENTEEN

THE wedding day…

Skye sat quietly in the white limousine as it was driven to the city centre. Opposite her sat Karin Holmes, the wedding planner Flavia had hired to ensure everything was done to perfection—a very pleasant woman who took all the angst out of getting things right. Skye was intensely grateful to her for all her instructions and advice.

Luc's mother sat beside Karin, facing Matt who was delighted to be riding in this very long car, chattering away to Nonna without the slightest sign of being nervous about this highly momentous occasion. His Nonna was clearly enjoying the conversation she was having with her grandson.

Skye reflected on how amazingly well Matt connected with both his grandparents. She had no worries about leaving him with them while she and Luc were away on their honeymoon, no worries about accepting Flavia's offer to collect Matt after school and mind him on the days she'd be at university this year, finishing her physiotherapy degree.

Luc had withdrawn his resignation and was staying on as head of his department in the Peretti Corporation. Where he truly belonged, Skye thought. And they'd purchased a house at Rose Bay, with a backyard for Matt to play in and a boathouse for the sailing yacht Luc wanted to buy. Living in his par-

ents' mansion, as Roberto had with his wife, was not
an option to be considered as far as Luc was concerned, much to Skye's relief.

It was only two months since Christmas and she
was still getting used to the turnaround from Luc's
father. She found Maurizio Peretti perhaps too much
like Luc in some ways. Once he set his mind on a
course, there were no holds barred. As Luc's fiancée,
she was treated like an honoured princess in public,
possibly an exercise in saving face. In private, he was
still getting to know her. Cautiously. Occasionally
testingly.

It had been the right decision to take the chance,
Skye thought with satisfaction. So much had changed
for the better. Luc was more relaxed now. She was
more relaxed. They were even going off on a honeymoon together. To Italy. The romantic island of
Capri.

And today she truly did feel like a bride. She loved
her dress—a stunning beaded gown in blush silk and
ivory French lace. With it, she'd bought a matching
beaded lace skullcap to sit over her forehead and
frame her face. Her hair was pulled back and woven
into elegant loops at the back, under which her veil
was cleverly attached to the cap—a wonderful long
veil that extended into a lace-edged train. Even her
shoes were special, high-heeled pearl sandals, glittering with the same beads used on the dress.

Flavia had taken her to her hair stylist, hired a
beautician to do her make-up, and a manicurist to buff
and varnish her nails with a dusky pink polish. 'A
perfect bride!' her future mother-in-law had happily
declared, looking Skye over before they'd stepped

into the limousine. Which was now pulling up outside St Mary's Cathedral.

No ordinary church for a Peretti marriage. No ordinary celebrant to conduct the ceremony, either. The Archbishop of Sydney was officiating, and inside were four hundred guests, many of whom were very prominent people far beyond the close Italian community that mainly formed the Peretti social circle. Skye had been amazed at some of the names on the wedding list.

It had struck her forcibly that this was what she was marrying into. This was Luc's heritage, what he would have given up for her—a nobody on any social scale. It also gave her more understanding of why his parents had been against the relationship, and how far they'd had to bend to accept that she was the woman Luc had chosen as his wife.

Background was important.

But love was more important.

Love was what held it all together, despite the differences.

Skye was very conscious of this as Karin Holmes helped her out of the car. Now that they were here, Luc's mother was to go ahead into the cathedral first, taking Matt with her. Skye gave her bouquet to Karin to hold and took Flavia's hands in hers, leaning forward to kiss her on the cheek.

'Thank you for all you have done for me. My own mother could not have done more,' she murmured gratefully.

'My dear…you do Luciano proud. You go to him now with my blessing. And his father's.'

* * *

Flavia Peretti left Skye to the wedding planner's competent handling, took her grandson's hand and entered the cathedral. Heads turned to watch the two of them walk down the aisle. She heard the whispers, knew tongues were wagging about Luciano's illegitimate child, but she refused to care what anyone thought.

Matteo was a wonderful little boy. She adored him. And she now had him firmly in her life. Perhaps more grandchildren, as well, further down the track—babies whose births could be celebrated with Luciano and Skye properly married. The empty future would be filled as she needed it to be filled.

She had no quarrel with Skye any more. Flavia was sure she would be a good daughter-in-law. Her giving nature made everything much easier than she had anticipated, thank God! And Maurizio…finally understanding what a husband should understand for his wife. It was all very well, being a big businessman and accumulating a great deal of wealth, living in a fine house, but without family…yes, he finally understood.

Maurizio Peretti smiled at the child who had walked into his life and grabbed his heart. Flavia seated them both beside him in the front pew, their grandson between them.

'Mummy looks beautiful, Nonno,' Matteo whispered.

'I think your Daddy looks fine, too,' he answered, nodding to where his son stood, waiting for his bride—the only bride he would accept.

A fine woman, too, Maurizio thought, intensely relieved that he had been wrong about Skye Sumner.

She would make a true life partner for Luciano, caring about his needs, just as Luciano cared about hers. It was also very generous of her to let the past go, not that Maurizio had meant to give her so much suffering. If her stepfather had been a decent man…though he himself had been wrong, very wrong in misjudging his own son's feelings, as well as Skye's.

Perhaps, he should acknowledge these things in his speech at the wedding reception. Nothing embarrassing, but a few words that expressed the real truth—a love that had already spanned many years, proving it was deep and steadfast, the best basis for a long, lasting and happy marriage. Although he and Flavia had done very well with hardly knowing each other before they were married. On the other hand, there had certainly been a spark between them—difficult to wait until their wedding night.

Luciano and Skye had not waited.

Yet how could he regret their having Matteo?

A fine grandson.

It was right to celebrate this marriage.

He would say so.

Luc was conscious of a sea of faces in front of him, hundreds of guests seated in the pews, waiting for the arrival of his bride. Undoubtedly it was an interesting occasion to them—Maurizio Peretti's eldest son marrying a woman who'd already borne his child. It was not interesting to him. It was vital. And every second of waiting was hell.

The last time he had been in this cathedral was for Roberto's funeral. Was his brother resting in peace now? Skye had been found. The child he hadn't known about was now a proudly acknowledged grandson. And he himself felt brilliantly alive again with Skye back in his world.

Smile, brother, he thought on a wave of love for the Roberto who had cared so much for him at the end. *The wrong has been righted.*

The boys' choir finished singing. The pipe organ started playing the first chords of Mendelssohn's Wedding March. At last, he thought, every nerve in his body electrified by the intense energy pouring from his need for Skye to be his wife.

His heart thundered in his chest as she began the walk down the aisle towards him—a vision of such loveliness his breath was caught in his throat. This is the woman I love, he told himself, not a dream. And she smiled her love at him, making the moment wonderfully real—Skye coming to him, his bride.

He no longer saw anyone else. He didn't even hear the music. His hand reached out for her and she took it—took his hand in marriage, for better and for worse, from this day forth. Luc didn't need to say the vows, didn't need to hear Skye say them. The big production his parents had wanted to make of this wedding meant nothing to him. Every bit of meaning in this ceremony was encased in the hand holding his.

A simple bonding…yet it meant they were one with each other.

It meant he and Skye owned a future together—a future no one could steal from them.

They were one.

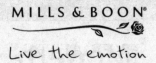

MIRA
An international collection of bestselling authors

EVER AFTER
by Fiona Hood-Stewart

**"An enthralling page turner—
not to be missed." —*New York Times*
bestselling author Joan Johnston**

**She belongs to a world of wealth,
politics and social climbing. But
now Elm must break away to find
happily ever after...**

Elm MacBride can no longer sit back and
watch her corrupt and deceitful husband's
ascent to power and his final betrayal sends her
fleeing to Switzerland where she meets
Irishman Johnny Graney. When her husband's
actions threaten to destroy her, Johnny must
save not only their love but Elm's life...

ISBN 07783 2078 2

Published 15th April 2005

MILLS & BOON

Summer days drifting away...

Summer Loving

VICKI LEWIS THOMPSON
RHONDA NELSON

On sale 3rd June 2005

Available at most branches of WHSmith, Tesco, ASDA, Martins, Borders, Eason, Sainsbury's and all good paperback bookshops.

FREE

4 BOOKS AND A SURPRISE GIFT!

We would like to take this opportunity to thank you for reading this Mills & Boon® book by offering you the chance to take FOUR more specially selected titles from the Modern Romance™ series absolutely FREE! We're also making this offer to introduce you to the benefits of the Reader Service™—

- ★ **FREE home delivery**
- ★ **FREE gifts and competitions**
- ★ **FREE monthly Newsletter**
- ★ **Books available before they're in the shops**
- ★ **Exclusive Reader Service offers**

Accepting these FREE books and gift places you under no obligation to buy; you may cancel at any time, even after receiving your free shipment. Simply complete your details below and return the entire page to the address below. You don't even need a stamp!

YES! Please send me 4 free Modern Romance books and a surprise gift. I understand that unless you hear from me, I will receive 6 superb new titles every month for just £2.75 each, postage and packing free. I am under no obligation to purchase any books and may cancel my subscription at any time. The free books and gift will be mine to keep in any case.

P5ZEE

Ms/Mrs/Miss/Mr...Initials ....
BLOCK CAPITALS PLEASE

Surname ....

Address ....

....

....Postcode ....

Send this whole page to:
The Reader Service, FREEPOST CN81, Croydon, CR9 3WZ